# THE GIN &
# CHOWDER CLUB

for Melissa

Hope you enjoy this
as much as I did.

Love, Mom

9/27/2020

# THE GIN &
# CHOWDER CLUB

## NAN ROSSITER

KENSINGTON BOOKS
www.kensingtonbooks.com

KENSINGTON BOOKS are published by

Kensington Publishing Corp.
119 West 40th Street
New York, NY 10018

All Kensington titles, imprints, and distributed lines are available at special quantity discounts for bulk purchases for sales promotion, premiums, fund-raising, educational, or institutional use.

Special book excerpts or customized printings can also be created to fit specific needs. For details, write or phone the office of the Kensington Special Sales Manager: Attn. Special Sales Department. Kensington Publishing Corp., 119 West 40th Street, New York, NY 10018. Phone: 1-800-221-2647.

Kensington and the K logo Reg. U.S. Pat. & TM Off.

ISBN-13: 978-0-7582-4667-7
ISBN-10: 0-7582-4667-6

First Kensington Trade Paperback Printing: June 2011
10  9  8  7  6  5  4  3  2  1

Printed in the United States of America

*For Bruce*

# PROLOGUE

Asa knelt down, picked up the envelope, and brushed away the sand. A sudden wind rushed down the beach and threatened to steal it from his hands, but he held it tightly and ran his fingers lightly over the familiar handwriting. The bittersweet memory of a summer long ago began to fill his mind like the gentle wave of an ebbing tide. Asa's heart raced as he turned the envelope over and slipped out its contents. Tucked inside a letter was a faded bus ticket dated June 21, 1961, and behind the ticket . . . an old photograph. Asa stared in disbelief. *I wondered what had become of this.* Tears filled his eyes as he remembered the night long ago. *She was so beautiful . . . and look at me . . . I was so young. . . .*

# PART I

*The revelation awaits an appointed time . . .*
*Though it linger, wait for it;*
*it will certainly come and will not delay.*

—Habakkuk 2:3

## ❧ 1 ❧

All day long, the leaden sky had hung low and threatening over Nauset Light. Asa sat at his desk and watched the lighthouse from his bedroom window. There was something haunting about the steady measurement in each revolution. . . . It was almost as if you could watch time passing.

"Asaaa, we could use your help down here," Samuel Coleman bellowed from the kitchen, interrupting his son's thoughts.

"Be right down," the boy answered. He scribbled one last sentence and closed the notebook, slipped it into the bottom of his desk drawer, and pushed back his chair, almost tripping over the family's old black Lab who was dozing on the braided rug beside his bed.

"Sorry, ole girl," Asa said, scratching her head.

Martha thumped her tail forgivingly and followed him gingerly down the worn narrow treads as he hurried to help his father and brother.

Samuel looked up. "Please rinse before dropping 'em in."

"Yes, Dad," the boys replied, rolling their eyes and elbowing each other. When they had first begun helping with the task of pulling clam bellies from their shells, the boys had stood side by side on a chair. They had grown considerably since then, but the task would not be the same if their father forgot to reiterate these mundane instructions. Asa didn't mind. He loved to help with the recipe that had been in their family for generations. He loved it not only because it was a tradition, but also because it meant that his parents would be having company. When they were younger, he and Isaac would already be in their pajamas when their parents' friends arrived, and they would be allowed to stay up just long enough to say hello and to explain that they had indeed helped with the chowder. Then they would be ushered upstairs for prayers and gently tucked into bed. The ocean breeze would whisper to them through their bedroom window as they listened to the merry laughter and voices downstairs. Finally, the boys would hear the chowder being served and the men jovially toasting, their voices lilting with unmistakable Cambridge accents. . . .

> " *'Tis the chowdah that waams a man's belly . . .*
> *But aye, 'tis the gin that waams his soul!"*

Then they would drift off to sleep, warmed by the happiness in their parents' deep old friendships. . . .

Asa pulled the last clam belly, gave it a quick rinse, and dropped it into the pot. He scooped the empty shells into a large metal pail, and Isaac carried it outside. Asa watched his father drain off the potatoes and add them to the steaming pot as well.

"So, what do you boys have planned for tonight?" Samuel asked as he poured in a generous amount of cream.

"Depends on the weather," Asa answered. "We're supposed to meet some of the fellows down on the beach for a bonfire."

"Just fellows?" His father looked up with raised eyebrows as Isaac came back into the kitchen.

"Dad, do you need ice up here?" Isaac asked.

"Yes, we'll need some ice. Are you offering to bring it up?"

"Sure. Asa, give me a hand."

Isaac gave his brother a playful shove as they headed out of the kitchen. Samuel watched them go. He was amazed to think that these young men were his sons. What had become of the small boys who, just yesterday it seemed, had relentlessly chased each other through the house? Where were the little fellows he had carried out into the waves, one in each arm, the older one squealing with delight, the younger one silent and wide-eyed with determined courage? Now they were as tall as he was.

Isaac and Asa were both slender and handsome. Isaac reminded Samuel of himself at the same age—chestnut-brown hair that was already showing signs of receding, hazel eyes, and long dark lashes that were the envy of every woman who ever saw them. Isaac was a mathematician and an artist. He was creative in a conscientious and orderly way. He attended art school in Rhode Island and, having just finished his foundation year, had settled on architecture as a major, and it suited him.

Asa, on the other hand, looked just like his mother. His features were gentle and kind. His blond hair shone in the sun. By August, it would be bleached to almost white against his brown skin. Asa's eyes were as blue as the sweet summer sky and often reflected the distant thoughts of the poet he tried to keep hidden. Samuel wondered why his younger son was so reluctant to share his writing but respected his privacy. Asa would be heading to college in the fall, and Samuel hoped that there, he would finally grow more confident.

Samuel's reverie was interrupted by the sound of chunks of

ice sliding into the old metal tub on the porch. The boys were laughing about something. Samuel decided that Isaac was teasing his brother again.

"Hey, Dad, are Uncle Nate and Noelle coming tonight?" Isaac asked through the open window.

"They are." Samuel nodded. He glanced at the clock and decided that it was late enough. He usually enjoyed having a cocktail when he was cooking, but today he had put it off. Now, with the chowder simmering on the ancient gas stove, Samuel went out onto the porch and handed Isaac his glass. His son filled it with ice cubes, splashed gin over the ice, topped it off with tonic, and squeezed a slice of lime into the mixture. He pushed the lime under the ice with his finger, gave it a quick stir, licked his finger, and handed the glass to his father.

"Nice stirrer," Samuel said as he took a sip and eyed his older son. "How'd you get so good at this?"

"Watchin' you," Isaac said with a mischievous smile.

As Samuel sat down on the wooden porch swing, the sun tried to break through the sullen clouds. A mild ocean breeze was pushing the clouds inland, and a bit of blue sky was finally visible. The old rambling Cape Cod house was situated on a bluff on the northern side of Nauset Light, and its back porch looked out over the vast expanse of the rugged shoreline that extended all the way to Coast Guard Beach. Asa leaned on the railing. He loved the ocean. When he and Isaac were younger, their father had told them that England was just over the horizon, and they had believed him. Soon after, Samuel had found them pushing off in their inflatable raft at low tide.

"We're going to England," they had shouted over the surf. "Tell Mom we'll be back for supper."

Samuel had had to swim out and pull them back in.

Both boys loved the ocean, but Asa was drawn to it in a deeper way and was captivated by the mystery of its deep waters. He was also fascinated by the faithful lighthouse that stood guard and prevailed against the region's punishing storms. On countless boyhood mornings, Asa had wandered down the worn path to the lighthouse's clearing on the precipice, slipped inside its heavy wooden door, climbed its narrow spiral stairs, studied its great rotating lens, and stood on a box to look out its tiny window to the sea. On just as many evenings, he had lain in bed and watched its light pass across the walls of the room he shared with his brother, dreaming of the day when he would live on the outer reaches of some jagged and treacherous coastline and *be* the trusted keeper of the light.

Now, Asa looked at the open window of the lantern room and thought of Noelle. She had stopped by that morning to drop off the old metal tub Nate had borrowed the previous summer. Asa had been the only one at home. He closed his eyes and pictured her standing in the doorway. . . .

"I can't stay," she had said.

"I know."

"It's so good to see you."

"It's good to see you too."

He had walked her to her car, and she had tried to think of something more to say. "I see they painted the lighthouse."

"Yeah, they've been working on that."

"You know, I've never been inside a lighthouse."

Asa had looked up at her in disbelief. "How can that be? Didn't you grow up in Maine?"

"Yes, but not coastal Maine."

He had reached for her hand. "C'mon, you have to see the inside."

"I can't . . ." She had pulled back, and he had let go. Seeing the disappointment in his eyes, she had relented. "Okay . . . but only for a minute."

"Only for a minute," Asa had agreed, smiling.

They had walked down the worn path, and Asa had jiggled the lock and pushed open the heavy door. When they reached the lantern room, Noelle had looked in amazement at the mechanics that created the light.

"It's a Fresnel lens," Asa had explained, showing her how the light was reflected. She had listened attentively and watched for a while before walking over to the window to look out at the sea. Asa had looked at the slender curve of her body outlined under her thin sundress and moved behind her. He had reached over her shoulder to push the window open, and the ocean breeze had rushed in and swept back her hair. Asa had slipped his arms around her, breathing in the lovely scent of her body, and Noelle had put her hands on his arms and closed her eyes. She had felt him against her and thought again about how easy it would be . . .

"Asa . . ."

"Don't . . ."

They had stood silently together. The only movement in the room had been the rotation of the reflecting light and the breeze that whispered in to cool their skin.

Finally, Noelle had broken the silence. "Asa, if you only knew how much I would love to be *with* you." She turned to him and searched his eyes. "I'm so sorry. . . . I should never have come." Asa had looked away, and Noelle had reached up and gently turned his face back to her, searching his eyes. "Asa, I would love to lie beside you. . . . Don't you see? But then what? What about Nate? I love him too. Asa, please, help me *not* let this happen. . . ."

Tears burned at Asa's eyes. "Noelle . . . don't *you* know?" He struggled with the words. "I would do *anything* you ask—anything at all—even if what you ask is *not* letting this happen. . . ."

Noelle had leaned up and pressed her lips against his flushed cheek. Asa had closed his eyes and kept his hands stiffly at his sides. . . .

"So, a bonfire with the fellows, is that it?" Samuel asked, interrupting Asa's thoughts.

Isaac winked at his brother. "That's the plan, Dad," he replied.

"Well, you boys know the rules—if you have any alcoholic beverages at your bonfire, stay out of the water," Samuel warned. "I was a fellow at a bonfire once, you know." He paused. "Are you going to hang around here for a while? I know everyone is looking forward to seeing you."

"Of course, Dad," said Asa. "We wouldn't miss out on chowder."

Samuel smiled and drummed his fingers on his glass. He looked his boys over. "Well, I hope you'll change out of those rag-tag shorts and T-shirts."

"Yup," said Isaac. "I might even take a shower."

"Sure you want to do that?" Asa teased. "It hasn't been a week yet."

Isaac gave his younger brother a smirk and walked toward the open door. Sarah Coleman was standing there with a grocery bag in her arms.

"Sam, I have the French bread and the shrimp if you want to come in and make cocktail sauce," she said. "Asa, maybe you could slice the bread."

"Yes, my dear," Samuel replied, easing himself up from the swing and walking over to freshen his drink.

"May I get you a cocktail . . . or would you like the whole rooster?"

Sarah smiled. "A small glass of white wine would be good."

Asa watched his parents. He was always amazed by the easy, warm comfort of their relationship. He wondered if he would ever know another so well . . . and if another could ever possibly know him. He thought of Noelle, and his heart ached for what could never be. He shook his head and went into the kitchen to slice the bread. Behind him, the summer sky was now a cloudless blue.

Nate peered in the bedroom doorway. "Almost ready, hon?"

"Almost." Noelle glanced in the mirror and sighed. *Why did God create wrinkles?*

Nate stepped into the room, wrapped his arms around her, and looked at her reflection too. She was slender, and her dark brown hair hung just past her shoulders. Her smooth skin was tan against the coral color of her linen sundress. She looked amazing and lovely, and Nate wondered how he hadn't noticed when he used to see her in her starched white nurse's uniform.

"How'd I get so lucky?" he pondered out loud.

Noelle put her hands on his arms and remembered how Asa had felt standing behind her.

She pushed the thought from her mind and whispered, "I'm the lucky one."

Nate closed his eyes and held her. The silver in his sideburns had long ago started spreading into the neatly clipped hair above his ears. Noelle had told him that it made him look distinguished, but he wasn't convinced. She continued to stroke his arms, pulling on his soft hair. She smelled his aftershave and felt a rush of warmth between her legs. Looking at Nate's head bent down over her shoulder, she thought about the events that had brought them to this place. Her eyes were drawn to the reflection of the bedroom behind them. She studied the Shaker headboard and the blue and white country quilt that was tucked neatly into its oak frame. She had found the bed in an antique shop, and it had fit perfectly between the two windows that overlooked the ocean. The walls were painted a soft sea green and were offset by creamy white trim and wainscoting that reached halfway up the walls. Noelle had chosen the colors and repainted the room soon after she and Nate had married. Even so, the memory of another life—Annie's life—still lingered. A gentle breeze drifted in through the windows and made the gingham curtains billow.

"We should go," Nate murmured.

"Mmm-hmm," she agreed, still lost in thought.

Annie, Nate's first wife, had died in this room. She had fought her long illness valiantly until its very end. As Annie's nurse, Noelle had witnessed the fight. She had witnessed the love and the heartache, and after Annie's passing, she had watched as grief and despair had consumed the brokenhearted man who was left behind. Witnessing all this and offering what comfort she could, Noelle Ryan couldn't help falling in love with Nathaniel Shepherd.

Blinded by sadness, however, Nate had barely noticed Noelle's presence, much less her striking features. It wasn't until they ran into each other some six months later that Nate noticed how beautiful she was. He had been going out of the grocery store as she was coming in. They had stopped to chat, and Nate had unexpectedly asked her if she had time for a cup of coffee. Noelle had obliged. They'd gone to a little outdoor café and continued their conversation, which Noelle had kept light. When they'd finished, Nate had leaned over to pick up his bag, and it had ripped open. Melted ice cream had dripped all over his shoes. "Guess I forgot what I had," Nate had said, laughing. It had felt good to laugh. After saying good-bye, he realized that he hadn't thought of Annie once during the conversation. It was a much-needed respite for his weary soul. Two weeks after their chance meeting, Samuel encouraged Nate to invite Noelle to one of their famous gatherings. He did, and by the end of the evening, it was evident to all present that Nate was smitten with Noelle, despite their eighteen-year age difference.

## ~ 3 ~

An hour later, Samuel was standing in the kitchen wearing a pressed white oxford, sleeves rolled to his forearms, and khaki slacks, mentally checking his list of preparations. Big band was playing on the radio. The kitchen counters were spotless. The shrimp was on ice, and the cocktail sauce had the perfect amount of fresh horseradish, Tabasco, Worcestershire, and lemon. The buttered French bread was in foil and waiting to go in the warm oven. The chowder was still simmering, and the fresh pepper grinder had been filled. The old metal tub was stocked with beer, white wine, tonic, and sweet tea on ice. Merlot, Tanqueray, and other mixers were on the old oak side table, and there were slices of lemon and lime in a chilled glass bowl. Sarah had cut blue hydrangea blossoms and made two bouquets, one for the kitchen and one for the porch. The outside table was covered with a pressed white linen cloth on which the glasses sparkled in the late afternoon sun. Samuel glanced around one last time. He prided himself on being an organized and conscientious host.

"Hey there, you old fox," a familiar voice called out.

Martha slowly pulled herself up off the wooden floor and barked warningly down the steps while her welcoming tail gave away her true emotions.

"Hey there, yourself!" Samuel replied, stepping out onto the porch and reaching for Nate's hand. The two friends clapped each other on the shoulder and hugged.

Samuel turned to Noelle. "I don't know how you put up with this old bear," he said, taking her hand and bringing it to his lips. "You are a saint—and a beautiful saint at that," he added with a wink.

Noelle smiled and blushed. "You two are a pair—you must have attended the same school of gallantry."

Samuel grinned back. "Actually, Nate learned everything he knows from me. So, in that regard, *you* are lucky!"

Martha continued to sniff and wiggle until Nate finally knelt down in front of her and held her head in his hands. "I didn't say hello to you, did I, ole girl?" he said, giving her a kiss on the nose. "You are getting as gray as I am."

Martha returned the kiss and, satisfied, went back to her spot in the sun.

Sarah came out and greeted her guests too. She'd grown fond of Noelle and gave her a warm hug. She then turned to Nate, and he took her hands and smiled at her. She leaned up and kissed him tenderly on the cheek. Sarah loved her husband's oldest friend and had prayed without ceasing while she watched his heart break. And now, although she dearly missed Annie's company, she was glad that Nate had found new happiness with Noelle.

Initially, Sarah had been skeptical of the romance. She was very protective of Nate and didn't want to see him endure any more heartache. But their relationship had unfolded gradually, and Sarah's concerns had eased. Finally, two years after Annie's passing, Nate announced that he and Noelle were getting married, and Samuel and Sarah had been very happy for them.

The two couples stood chatting when Isaac appeared at the door.

"Well, here he is!" Nate smiled. "Come on out and let's see the college boy."

Isaac stepped out and shook Nate's hand. "Hey, Uncle Nate," he said, grinning. Then he turned and kissed Noelle on the cheek.

"So, how's Providence?" Nate asked. "Did you have a good year?" He glanced at Isaac's attire: stone-colored shorts, white polo, and black canvas high-top sneakers. "Looks like that crazy art community didn't have too much effect on you." Isaac nodded with a smile, and Nate looked up and noticed that Asa was standing at the door. "And here's the other trouble-maker!"

Asa couldn't help but smile as he pushed open the door. He had showered and changed, too, and he had the same casual look as his brother except that his high-tops were white, and his polo was a faded cobalt blue that matched his eyes. He wore a Red Sox cap, which, when new, had been cream-colored with a navy visor and a deep red *B*; now it was frayed and faded, and even though he had a new cap, he always wore his old favorite.

Asa politely greeted his parents' friends just as his brother had, with a firm handshake and a kiss. He lightly brushed Noelle's cheek with his lips and slowly breathed in her familiar fragrance. He closed his eyes and clenched his jaw; he was becoming well versed in the art of concealment.

"Look at these fine young men!" Nate exclaimed. "Sam, you homely old fellow, how did you manage to have such handsome sons?"

"Thank goodness Sarah had something to do with it," Samuel replied, smiling. "Isaac, how'd you like to fix our guests some drinks?" Then he added, "Please use a proper stirrer this time." He turned to Nate. "You have to watch him—he has an unconventional way of stirring."

Nate nodded. "So, what're you boys up to this summer?"

Isaac answered as he made their drinks. "I'm going into town with Dad during the week to help out in the shop and hopefully learn a little bit about interior architecture."

Samuel shook his head and eyed his older son. "It's not as innocent a plan as it sounds. As usual, there's a woman involved."

Nate raised his eyebrows. "A college woman, I'm sure," he said, winking at Isaac as he was handed his drink. Isaac just grinned. Nate then turned to Asa, who was leaning on the railing. "And how 'bout you, Asa? Any women—I mean *work*—in your summer plans?"

Asa laughed and avoided looking at Noelle. "I'm working down at the coast guard station, repairing sills and painting."

Samuel shook his head again. "Don't be fooled. His plans aren't innocent either," he teased. "He'll have a bird's-eye view of all the girls on the beach. That's why he likes that job so much."

Asa just smiled and looked away. Both boys were accustomed to the good-natured teasing by their father and Nate.

"Well, Asa," Nate said thoughtfully, "if you don't get enough of that sort of work over at the coast guard station, I'm looking for someone reliable to repair a couple of sills and do some painting at the house. If you're interested, let me know."

Asa nodded. Just then, Martha struggled to her feet and started barking again. Other guests were arriving, and Martha, who was the self-appointed head of the welcoming committee, was ready, tail wagging.

By eight o'clock, Asa and Isaac had said good night to their parents' friends. Earlier in the day, they had loaded Asa's old Chevy pickup with driftwood and beach chairs. "Do we have everything?" Isaac asked as he put two coolers, one empty, the other full of ice, behind the tailgate.

"No," Asa said, and ran back up the stairs. He grabbed his notebook and pen and stuffed them into his shoulder bag before heading back down. He pushed open the screen door just as Noelle, with an empty bowl in one hand, reached to pull it open. He held the door for her, and they stepped back into the shadow of the kitchen.

"Are you going out?" she asked with surprise.

"For a little while . . ." He paused and gave her a mischievous grin. "Want to come?"

Noelle looked around. "Mmm . . . I'd love to. . . ." Her eyes sparkled, and Asa stepped closer. "You aren't making this easy," she said quietly. "I thought you were going to help—"

"I'm trying to help," he said softly, "but there's just something about you."

The sound of the screen door made them quickly step apart. Samuel and Nate came into the kitchen looking for the limes, and Nate gave Noelle a puzzled look.

Samuel, seeing that Asa hadn't left yet, repeated his warning. "Remember what I said."

"Yes, Dad," Asa replied.

"And let me know about that extra work," Nate reminded him. "Don't let your father tell you otherwise. I *do* pay on time."

Asa laughed. "I guess I could use the extra money. Dad keeps mumbling about having two tuitions."

"All right, then," Nate replied. "Maybe you could come by tomorrow so I can show you which windows need the most attention."

"All right, I'll come by," Asa said, shaking Nate's hand.

Samuel gave his son a hug. "Love you . . . Behave." Then he added, "Tell your brother too."

"I will," Asa replied. "Love you, too, Dad." He caught Noelle's eye and smiled as he went out the door.

"Twelve o'clock!" Samuel shouted after him.

"Okay," they heard him answer from outside.

"It's damn hard lettin' them go," Samuel said, shaking his head.

Nate put his hand on Samuel's shoulder. "You've done a great job, Sam," he consoled. "I wish I'd had the chance."

"You never know," Samuel said, taking the replenished bowl from Noelle. He smiled and winked at her. "Miracles *do* happen."

Nate laughed. "It *would* take a miracle—not to mention I'm much too old for such nonsense!" Nate turned to look at Noelle, knowing she would love nothing more than to have a family. She returned a sad half-smile but didn't say anything as she stepped outside while the two men lingered in the kitchen.

Noelle slipped through the gathering of friends and made her way over to the railing to look out at the waves. What Nate had said was true—she would love nothing more than to have a child. It was her deepest prayer. She looked at the sky, which had become a radiant blaze of pink and orange, and then turned to watch the lighthouse continue its steady, assiduous rhythm.

## 4

Asa pulled the truck into the parking lot of the package store, and Isaac climbed out. "Get bottles!" Asa called after him. Isaac came out and put the beer into the empty cooler. He poured some of the ice on top and then pushed the Tanqueray and tonic into the ice of the other cooler.

"Damn, I forgot a lime," Isaac said. "We're going to have to make another quick stop."

"Bet you forgot cups too," Asa said. "I don't know why you have to drink something so complicated."

"Someone has to carry on the family tradition."

Asa just shook his head.

Fifteen minutes later, the boys pulled into the parking area at Nauset Light. They were greeted with cheers and jeers by their small circle of friends, people they had spent every childhood summer with—most whose parents were at the gathering back at the house. The cheering was because they had finally arrived, the jeering because they were late. Isaac got out of the truck and shook hands with the fellows and gave hugs to the girls. There had been a time when Samuel had worried that his sons did not interact enough with other children. In most group situations, they had always tended to stay together, and even in Sunday school, Asa had always wanted to tag along to Isaac's class.

Isaac had said, "Don't worry, Dad. Asa's my wingman."

Samuel had laughed. And he need not have worried, because as soon as they became teenagers, Isaac and Asa seemed to have no trouble interacting with others.

Asa sat in the truck, grinning. "All right, we brought the wood. You guys get to carry it down those stairs." They all knew what he meant. The bluff overlooking Nauset Light Beach was straight down, and one trip up the stairs was a workout. It would take several trips to carry down all of the wood.

"Maybe there's enough down there already," someone offered.

"Oh, don't be a slouch," Asa teased. "I run up those forty-seven steps all the time."

It was true. Asa loved to run. On most days, he ran from the lighthouse to the coast guard station. He would return with a goal of running the stairs four times, although he would sometimes change his mind after three. On other days, he would ride his bike down Ocean View Drive, leave it at the coast guard station, and run farther down the beach, past the weather-beaten two-room structure the locals called the Outermost House. Asa knew the history of the little house, but he preferred to call it the Fo'c'sle, just as its original owner had. This sun-bleached structure that sat in front of Nauset Marsh had been built by a local carpenter in the late spring of 1925 for author and naturalist Henry Beston. Beston, who referred to himself as the "Vagabond of the Dunes," had then spent a year weathering the coastal storms of Cape Cod and living in solitude. He had chronicled his experience in a book called *The Outermost House*. The slim volume had captivated Asa, and he drew inspiration from its descriptive passages of secluded life, buffeted between the relentless forces of nature and the serenity of observing the gradual change of seasons. When Asa ran past the house, he could almost picture Beston sitting out front, becoming as much a part of the landscape as the tall sea grass swaying on the dunes. Oh, what an experience it must have been!

Asa climbed out of the truck and slung his bag over his shoulder. He reached under the dash for his bottle opener, slipped it into his pocket, walked to the back of the truck, and pulled down the tailgate.

"If you all take two or three pieces, you might have to make only a couple of trips," he said teasingly while he pulled out his cooler and chair and headed for the stairs. He started to walk away but then smiled, turned around, and came back to grab two big pieces of wood.

Before long, the group had a good fire going. They lounged in beach chairs, and Isaac made a round of gin and tonics for anyone who was interested. The boys in the group toasted life, using their fathers' legendary gin and chowder toast, and, after a while, several in the group decided to go for a walk along the water. When it turned out that everyone was going, Asa decided to stay behind.

"I'll just stay here and keep an eye on the fire," he said.

"Sure you don't mind?" Isaac asked.

"*You* know I don't mind."

In fact, Asa couldn't have been happier. As the group started off, shouting and waving good-bye to him, Asa waved back, laughing at them and pulling his cooler closer to his chair. He slipped out an icy bottle, opened it, leaned back in his chair, and took a long drink. He watched the fire for a while and then fished around in his shoulder bag for his notebook. Asa never minded being alone. Sometimes he thought he could spend his entire life alone—a recluse, like Beston or Thoreau.

He watched the sparks of embers shooting up into the darkness and listened to the pounding of the waves. He looked at the moon and its reflection on the water. And then Asa looked higher and watched the red and white beams of the lighthouse circling endlessly in the night sky, and he wondered what Noelle was doing at that very moment. . . .

## 5

Both Samuel and Nate came from Boston families, and each had inherited businesses that were generations old. Eli Coleman, Samuel's father, had turned the reins of Coleman & Son Fine Woodworking over to Samuel early on so that he could "retire and spend more time fishing." But for many years after, Samuel would arrive to open up the shop and find Eli already there, smiling and ready to "keep an eye on things." Eli had been a beloved grandfather to Asa and Isaac, and even though he had died almost eight years ago, he was still deeply missed.

Eli's father had been Josiah, and it was he who had built the post-and-beam barn that later became "the shop." Out of wood he crafted any items that were needed by his neighbors: rocking chairs, window frames, mantels, cupolas, and, of course, cabinets. His reputation for excellent craftsmanship spread throughout the area, and before long, he was crafting, almost exclusively, custom cabinetry for the finest homes in Boston.

About this same time, Nate's grandfather, Abe Shepherd, had started an accounting firm for upscale businesses in the

Boston area. Because of his name, everyone assumed Abe to be trustworthy. His reputation and his business grew, so when Josiah Coleman's woodworking business started to bring in more income than he could manage, he decided to seek the services of someone who knew about such matters. His customers recommended Abe Shepherd.

When Abe and Josiah shook hands for the first time, the conversation that followed seemed more like a reunion of two old friends than of two newly acquainted businessmen. Abe and Josiah found that they had a great deal in common, and as their meeting drew to a close, they agreed to meet again in a more social setting. The following Friday evening, they met in Haymarket for drinks. Hungry after a long day, they also ordered chowder, and the conversation turned to old family recipes. After much good-natured wrangling, it was decided that a contest was in order. Abe suggested that Josiah bring his wife and young son out to his family's summerhouse in Orleans. Josiah agreed. The two men would cook for their wives and have the ladies judge who made the best chowder.

As it turned out, the women loved both the men's efforts and couldn't decide between them. Abe and Josiah reluctantly conceded that both chowders were indeed delicious. They decided to try combining the ingredients of the two recipes, and the resulting creation was rich and creamy and full of clams— and became the legendary chowder recipe. The social gatherings of the two families and their friends became known as the Gin and Chowder Club.

Spending time at the Shepherds' summerhouse, Josiah and his wife fell in love with the ocean and decided to find a place of their own. After looking at several old homes, they finally settled on a rambling center-chimney Cape overlooking the rugged coast in nearby Eastham. The house had a commanding view of the shoreline and of the neighboring lighthouse. This view had been the real selling point, because the house itself, although charming, was weathered and in great need of repair. Its rambling yard was enclosed by a broken picket fence whose main support was an overgrown wild rosebush that was covered with a profusion of pink blossoms. The old-fashioned gardens surrounding the house also reflected years of neglect, but a plethora of blue hydrangea bushes, daylilies, black-eyed Susan, and bee balm made it evident that someone had once cared very much. Despite the house's run-down appearance, Josiah and his wife saw only potential and bought it without a second thought.

In the years that followed, it was only natural that, growing up together and spending summers on the Cape, Josiah Coleman's son Eli and Abe Shepherd's son Lincoln would forge a friendship of their own and would later carry on the businesses and traditions of their fathers. These were eventually passed down to their sons Samuel and Nate.

## 6

Nate and Noelle arrived home shortly before eleven. In the old days, Nate recalled, the gatherings had lasted until the early hours of the morning. The group had been a little wilder back then too. Now they were all slowing down. *Ah, well, they were all a little wiser too,* he thought.

As they pulled into the sandy drive that wound into the secluded setting, Noelle looked up at the silhouette of the house's bowed roof and its massive center chimney. They had forgotten to leave on an outside light, but the full moon brightly illuminated the grounds and pool.

"How 'bout a swim?" Noelle asked.

Nate laughed. "It's a bit late, don't you think?"

"C'mon, it'll feel good," Noelle said. "I'll even wear your favorite outfit."

"That's very tempting," Nate replied, "but you must remember—you're married to an old man."

Nate parked the car, and they walked toward the back garden. Noelle reached for Nate's hand. "Well, perhaps you can get a towel for me, then," she said, not willing to give up so easily.

"That," he replied, "I can do."

When Nate returned with a towel, he saw Noelle's dress draped over the wooden gate. Inside the gate, dropped enticingly along the stone patio, was a trail of undergarments.

"I have your towel, miss," he called.

"Thank you, sir. And by the way, it's 'Mrs.'," she called from the far end of the pool. She was standing on the diving board in the moonlight, and he took it all in, feeling himself become aroused.

"It's definitely the quiet ones you have to look out for," he said to himself.

"What's that?" she called.

"Just remembering how prim and proper I once thought you were," Nate called back, sitting on a lounge chair. Noelle dove into the pool without even a splash. She came up and slowly swam toward him.

"But I am prim and proper—for a married woman," she said, standing up in the shallow end, streams of water cascading down her smooth skin.

"Where in the world are your tan lines?" Nate asked, his eyes playing over every inch of the view, his mind loving every word of the playful banter.

"You don't get any when you have such a private sunny spot," she replied. "Are you sure you won't join me?"

"I'm sure. I don't want to get wet," he said, smiling. "I'll dry, though—when you're ready, of course." He hoped her swim wasn't over. "How 'bout a few more dives? I'd be happy to judge them."

"I'm sure you would," she said, arching her back and stroking toward the other end.

Nate watched her as he unbuttoned his shirt, revealing the

soft curly silver hair that covered his lean chest and abdomen. He was not ashamed of the shape he was in. In fact, for fifty, he thought he was pretty trim. He leaned back in his chair and loosened his pants. Noelle stepped onto the diving board. She reached her arms straight over her head, completely uninhibited, and dove smoothly again.

When she came up, Nate teased her. "Nine and a half. Always room for improvement—better try again."

She laughed and dove in a couple more times. Finally, Nate said, "Now, that was perfect."

Noelle swam to the steps and walked toward him. Nate held the towel open, and Noelle just stood in front of him. He slowly dried her legs and abdomen and just enjoyed looking. He reached up to softly dry her breasts, and Noelle watched his eyes. She slipped her leg over the lounge chair, and Nate leaned back. He dropped the towel to the ground, slid his hands onto her hips, and gently pulled her down. She moved slowly back and forth, teasing him. Together they watched the slow movement between their bodies until Noelle caught her breath.

"You're wrong," he murmured. "I'm the lucky one."

## ⁓ 7 ⁓

Asa was up early the next morning. In the gray half-light, he glanced over at his brother. Even though they had been home before midnight, they hadn't gotten much sleep; instead, they had lain on their beds and talked into the night. Isaac was torn between an old love named Jen from summers past and a new one he had met in college. Jen had been at the beach the night before, and seeing her again had rekindled the flame. Isaac's new love, due to absence, had lost the advantage. Asa could offer little advice. He had always believed that if a person truly loved another, there could be no one else, but now he wasn't so sure. Is it possible to love two people?

Asa silently pulled on his shorts and went downstairs. Martha was curled up on her bed, but when she saw Asa, she thumped her tail and rolled onto her back to have her belly scratched. Asa obliged and then let her out and fed her. He left a note saying that he had done so, gave her a kiss on the head, and quietly slipped outside. A fog had rolled in during the night, and Asa could only see the shaft of light from the light-house slicing through the mist. He pulled his T-shirt over his head, stretched, and jogged slowly down the road toward the beach. As he trotted down the steps, he couldn't see the water; he could only hear the waves. The ocean air was thick and heavy with moisture. He recalled how clear and bright the night before had been and couldn't believe what a difference a few hours made. As he headed toward the hard, wet sand along the water's edge, he passed the dark, smoldering site of their fire and thought of the tranquility of sitting there alone, remembering. Now, as he ran, he allowed his mind to replay the memory again. . . .

He thought about the moment he had realized that he was attracted to Noelle. When Annie had died, he was just a boy, but in the years that followed, Noelle had become a part of Nate's life, a friend to his parents, and had always been someone he could talk to. He had simply loved to be around her, and she had always made time for him; as he matured, so had their friendship. They had certainly never planned for anything to happen, but then one evening last spring, Asa had stopped in to say good-bye before returning to school, and Noelle had been home alone. They had talked for a while, until Asa had said he'd better go. He had kissed her—as he always did. But this time it had lasted a moment longer, and it had felt like something more. When they had finally stepped apart, Noelle had looked startled, and Asa had felt his heart pounding. Noelle had looked at him intently and had lightly touched his cheek, and then to his astonishment she had leaned up and kissed him again.

Asa continued to run, watching the fog slowly lifting. He tried to push the memory from his mind. *I must stop remembering. I can't think this way.* But it seemed that they had already stumbled down a path that allowed no return. Finally, Asa just pushed himself to run as hard as he could and tried to convince himself that he preferred the simplicity of solitude.

\* \* \*

When Asa got back to the house, his father was up and making coffee.

"How 'bout some of my world-famous blueberry pancakes?" he asked.

"Sounds good," Asa replied as he poured a splash of orange juice into his ice water. "Do I have time to take a shower?"

"You do if you're quick—and see if you can rouse your brother too."

Sarah came into the kitchen in her bathrobe. "Mmmm, coffee. I knew I married you for a reason," she said, smiling at Samuel. As usual, Sarah had waited up for the boys, even though Isaac had insisted it wasn't necessary.

"After all," he had said, "no one worries when I'm at college."

"If you only knew," she had replied.

This morning, however, she was glad to have everyone home and safe. She gave hugs to her two men who were up and about, filled her coffee cup, and went out onto the porch with her Bible. For as long as Asa could remember, this had been his mother's early morning routine. He knew that he was among her prayers, and it always gave him a funny, warm feeling.

After breakfast and showers, the Coleman boys were pressed, dressed, and ready for church. Isaac and Asa had learned early on that Sunday mornings were set aside for God, and even though they would have much rather gone hiking or exploring, their mother was unyielding when it came to church and Sunday school. So, Isaac and Asa were "regulars," and by the time they could read, they knew their way around the Bible better than most adults. By ages four and five, they had sat obediently in the church pew between their parents and, with their eyes squeezed tightly shut, whispered the Lord's Prayer. By eight and nine, they could both recite all of the books of the Old and New Testaments, as well as Psalms 23, 91, and 121. Sarah was proud of her boys' knowledge and believed strongly in the verse from Proverbs, "Train up a child in the way he should go, and when he is old he will not depart from it."

Samuel agreed with this, but he also wanted his boys to have a growing, living faith, one on which they could always rely. He wanted their lives to have purpose, and he wanted them to use their talents and passions to glorify God. He had repeatedly impressed this upon them. As they grew older, however, he could only pray that they had absorbed some of his guiding doctrines.

Asa sat in the pew next to Isaac and looked out the tall window. He had always marveled at the height and number of panes in the old mullioned windows. The architecture was typical of a New England Congregational church. It had been built in the mid-1700s and had originally served as a meetinghouse as well. Since its establishment, there had been several renovations. In the 1800s, the first change was made when a center aisle had been added. At the same time, the pews had been curved so that the central focus was on the pulpit, the Bible— God. The interior decoration was minimal, almost stark in its simplicity. In front of the pulpit stood a Communion table and beside it, a matching baptismal font. There was no cross, which bothered Sarah, but because this was her church only in the summer and occasionally during the rest of the year, she did not make it an issue. When it wasn't communion Sunday, there was always an arrangement of freshly cut flowers on the table. Today, there was a bouquet of deep purple lilac blossoms from someone's garden. On either side of the heavy, fragrant blossoms, two tall white tapers flickered. Asa found the simplicity to be striking.

As they stood to sing the opening hymn, "God of Grace and God of Glory," Asa noticed Nate and Noelle standing two rows in front of them and remembered his promise to stop by that afternoon. His mind drifted from the service, and he was relieved when the benediction was finally delivered. He was far too preoccupied with his own thoughts to be able to benefit from the sermon. The boys stood with their parents and shook hands with the other parishioners. Nate and Noelle made their way over too. Samuel and Sarah chatted with them, and Asa arranged with Nate to stop by after lunch.

Back at the house, Asa and Isaac hurried upstairs to change. Samuel had suggested BLTs for lunch, which happened to be the boys' specialty. They came down to the kitchen, and while they made the sandwiches and heated up the leftover chowder, they planned their afternoon. Martha sat patiently at Asa's feet while he turned the bacon.

"Don't worry, ole girl, I'm cooking one just for you," Asa said, scratching her behind the ears and stirring soup at the same time.

Isaac rinsed and sliced two tomatoes. "So, we'll meet you at Nauset around two o'clock. Does that sound good?" Nauset Beach was in Orleans, and its close proximity to Nate and Noelle's house would make it easy for Asa to come down when he was done. Nauset and Coast Guard Beach, with its long sandbars, had always been their two favorites for swimming.

Isaac continued. "I guess I'll call Jen—I told her that I would—and I'll see who else is around." Isaac put the bread in the toaster and lamented, "I am beginning to wish that I wasn't going in to Boston with Dad during the week."

Asa turned the stove off and laid the bacon out on a paper towel to drain. He wished Isaac was going to be around, too, but he didn't let on.

"Oh, it won't be so bad," he replied, breaking off a big piece of bacon and giving it to Martha. "Careers before women, remember?"

"Yeah, that's easy for you to say," Isaac teased.

## 8

Asa considered walking around back after parking his truck but then decided to knock at the front door instead. Asa and Isaac had spent almost as much time at Uncle Nate's house as they had at their own. They had slept over on countless occasions, and although they preferred swimming in the ocean, they had also spent countless hours in the pool. Nate always teased that they were going to wear out the water. Annie had loved having them over for a swim. She had taught them how to dive and how to swim all the way to the bottom to retrieve a shiny penny. If Sarah had some shopping to do, Annie had always been willing to "spend time with her boys." She'd never called it babysitting. Instead, she would give them her undivided attention and loved to be challenged to a game of Parcheesi or Scrabble. Sometimes they would make ice-cream sodas or cookies, and then they would sit out on the porch and munch or slurp while Annie read stories to them about pirates and shipwrecks. While she read, Asa and Isaac would lie back on the cushioned wicker furniture and look out at the ocean until

they could no longer keep their eyes open. Asa had often wondered why Annie and Nate didn't have any children.

Asa loved Nate's old house almost as much as the memories.
As a boy, he thought that the wood-shingled bow roof looked
like an upside-down ship. The house was sided in the traditional style of Cape Cod. It had painted clapboard on the front
and weathered gray shingles on the ends and on the back. As
Asa walked to the front door, he noticed that the deep red paint
on the trim was peeling, as was the paint on the clapboard. The
front door was original: stained oak, solid and heavy. Asa lifted
the old circular iron knocker and tapped it. Noelle answered almost immediately.

"Asa, you don't have to knock," she said, inviting him in.
"*You* know you can just come in."

Asa half smiled. "I wish that were so. . . ."

She studied his eyes. "Nate is on the back porch," she said
quietly.

Asa nodded and looked over her shoulder, his heart suddenly pounding. He reached for her hand and pulled her toward him. To his surprise, she didn't resist. He felt the curve of
her body fit naturally into his and lightly traced the outline of
her low-cut blouse. He kissed her softly until they heard movement on the porch. Noelle quickly pulled away and shook her
head in disbelief.

She turned toward the kitchen and said loudly, "I have a
peach cobbler in the oven, but it's not quite ready. Would you
like some iced tea?"

"Sounds good," Asa murmured, leaning against the door
and waiting to regain his composure before following her.

Nate looked up over his glasses. "Hey there," he said, standing and putting down the Sunday paper.

"Hey, Uncle Nate," Asa said, shaking his hand. Nate motioned to a chair. Asa looked around and noticed that the cushions still had the same soft fabric he had fallen asleep on as a boy. He smiled—he had always thought that this porch was one of the most pleasant spots on Earth. It was screened in, and no matter how hot the day, there was always a cool ocean breeze drifting through. It was spacious and had several sitting areas: cushioned wicker chairs that circled a glass cocktail table, a small dining table with wooden chairs in the corner overlooking the ocean, and a long wooden swing on the far end, just like the one at home. Finally, hanging year-round from the ceiling was a string of small white Christmas lights that sparkled at night and gave the porch a festive look, even when there wasn't a party.

Asa sat down, and Noelle brought out a tray with a pitcher of iced tea and glasses on it. She poured a glass for each of them and handed one to Asa.

"Thanks," he said.

"You're welcome," she replied, a little too quickly, and handed the other glass to Nate.

"Well, Asa," Nate started, "Noelle and I have been talking, and we don't want you to feel pressured into this job. If you change your mind and decide that you have more going on than you can handle, please just say so. We'll certainly understand."

Asa nodded. "Well, I'd like to give it a try and see how it goes. I'll tell you if it's too much."

Nate looked at Noelle. "All right, then," he said. He turned back to Asa. "You probably noticed that the front of the house is peeling. Ideally, we'd like to have it scraped and repainted. It's not very high, so I think a stepladder will be sufficient. The sills out there are in pretty good shape, but the trim is also peeling and needs to be scraped and repainted. I painted the trim on the ends of the house last summer, so they are fine, but there are three sills in the back that, between the weather and the ocean air, constantly take a beating. You can get to them from the roof of the porch," he said, pointing up. "I don't know if they need to be replaced or if they can just be painted and last another season." He hesitated. "Why don't we go take a look?"

Asa put down his glass and followed Nate up the narrow stairs. Growing up, he and Isaac had often played hide-and-seek in this house. No rooms had ever been off-limits, so Asa knew every closet, corner, and hiding spot. However, he had not been upstairs since before Annie died. As he climbed the worn treads, he was overwhelmed by a rush of memories. Asa stepped into the bedroom and immediately noticed that the room had been painted. He also realized that the old canopy bed and matching furniture had been replaced. The last time he had stood in this room was when Sarah had brought them over to visit Annie. At the time, Isaac and Asa had not realized the importance of their visit; they had not known that their mother had brought them over to say good-bye. Instead, they had thought that their dear friend was going to get better and invite them over again to play cards, or read, or swim. They had sat on the bed and held her hands; they had laughed with her and told her all of their latest adventures; and then they had kissed her on the cheek and said, "See you soon, Ole Pie," just as they always had, and hopped down the stairs.

A week later, Uncle Nate had come to the house with tears streaming down his drawn cheeks. Asa had felt a scary, tight knot in his stomach. *Why was Uncle Nate crying?* Sarah had hugged Nate and cried too. Then he had turned to kneel down in front of the boys and quietly told them that Annie had died. At first, Isaac hadn't believed him. He told Nate that he had just seen her and that she was fine. Asa had just stood there, his fists clenched, his eyes stinging. He was bewildered at his brother's disbelief, at Nate's tears—and his mother's tears too. He ran to her, and she had just held him tightly.

Asa was overwhelmed by the sudden memory of all this. Nate turned and looked back and saw Asa's eyes glistening. "I guess you haven't been up here in a while," he said.

"Yeah," Asa said quietly.

"I miss her too," Nate said, putting his hand on Asa's shoulder. "The old furniture is in the guest bedroom." Then he turned back to the window and pushed it up as high as it would go and took the screen out. He leaned it against the dresser. "How are you with heights?" he asked. "It's not too bad out here—and the view is great!" They stood on the roof looking out over Nauset Beach, and Asa mentioned that he was meeting Isaac there later.

Nate replied, "I guess we better hurry up, then. Noelle made a peach cobbler just because you were coming, and she'll be upset if you don't have time to have some."

Nate pointed to the sills, and they decided that at least one of them would need to be replaced. Asa described to Nate how they were doing the job at the coast guard station, and Nate felt confident that Asa would have no problem replacing it. He told him that he had an account at the hardware store and to charge whatever supplies he needed. When they came back into the kitchen, Noelle was just dishing out the cobbler. She looked up and smiled gently. Asa returned the smile and longed to hold her again.

"It's even better with vanilla ice cream," Nate said, opening the freezer.

"Sounds good," Asa managed softly.

They sat out on the porch and visited a while more. Nate asked Asa how his last year at the Gunnery had been and reminded him that it was his alma mater too. Asa answered that the year had gone well; he had been fourth in his class, and if it hadn't been for calculus, he probably would have been salutatorian. It was quiet for a minute, and then Noelle asked him if he was looking forward to college. Asa looked at her and nodded thoughtfully before feeling the need to look away. He suddenly realized that his feelings about going away had changed. Noelle commented that Hanover was a pretty little town and that she loved the White Mountains.

Asa watched the easy way Nate and Noelle interacted with each other and felt a wave of jealousy sweep through him.

He picked up his glass and plate, and stood. "Well, I better get going. The cobbler was great. Thanks." He smiled at Noelle.

She and Nate stood too. Noelle took the plate and glass from his hands. "You can leave those," she said.

Nate looked at Noelle. "Well, my dear, what days are you working now?" he asked.

"Tuesday, Wednesday, and Friday," she replied, "but Asa can come anytime."

Nate followed Asa to the door. "Well, there you go. If Noelle's not here, the key is under the mat. Also, feel free to use the pool and help yourself to whatever you can find in the fridge—really, Asa, just make yourself at home. Oh, and make sure you keep track of your time."

"Okay," Asa replied as he backed down the steps.

As Asa pulled away, Nate put his arm around Noelle and teasingly whispered in her ear, "So much for no tan lines."

Noelle just nodded, her heart suddenly filled with an odd sadness. . . .

## 9

The boys returned from the beach late in the afternoon. Samuel and Sarah were sitting together on the porch swing enjoying a cold glass of sweet tea and talking about the week ahead. Sarah was accustomed to spending much of the summer on the Cape without Samuel, but she still missed him when he returned to their home in Boston. It had always been this way: she and the boys spending the long, leisurely summer months at the Cape house and Samuel coming and going as his schedule allowed.

Martha thumped her tail happily when she heard the boys on the steps.

"Well, how was it?" their father asked.

"Great," Isaac answered as they hung their beach towels over the railing and sat down.

Sarah looked at their sandy legs and feet. "Please don't go in the house until you've rinsed off," she warned.

"Yes, Mom," they replied, smiling. It was just like being told by their father to rinse the clams before adding them to the chowder. The boys had been rinsing themselves off in the cool outdoor shower after a day at the beach for as long as they could remember. When they were toddlers, Sarah had always ushered them around back for a quick rinse and then let them run innocently around the porch naked until they were dry. Those days were long gone, but still, their mother felt it necessary to remind them.

"Isaac, are you all packed?" Samuel asked. "I'd like to head into town tonight."

"I'm not, but it won't take long," he replied. "Dad, do you know when we'll be coming back out?"

"Probably not till Friday. Why? Are you already having second thoughts?"

"No . . . well . . . maybe." Isaac hesitated. "I'd just like to be able to spend some time out here."

"I'm sure you'll have plenty of time out here, Isaac. Why don't you wait and see how it goes before you start worrying?"

"All right," he said, standing and pulling off his T-shirt. He headed around the house to rinse off his legs before going upstairs.

Samuel turned to Asa. "And how'd it go for you? Does the work at Nate and Noelle's seem manageable?"

"Mmm-hmm." Asa nodded.

"Do you know when you'll start?"

Asa stopped stroking Martha's head and leaned back in his chair. "I think I'll try to start on Tuesday." Martha put her paw up on Asa's leg and gave his hand a nudge with her nose. Asa absently put his hand back on her head, and she contentedly closed her eyes again.

"I think they're pleased that you are willing to help with this and that they can count on you," Samuel remarked.

"And *I'm* sure Noelle will like having someone around," Sarah added. "I don't think she likes being at the house alone all week. She misses Nate and has said she'd rather just come out on the weekends with him. She told me this is going to be the last summer she works out here and that she is hoping to change her position in Boston to year-round."

Samuel nodded thoughtfully as he got up to check the charcoal. "She won't have any trouble either. She's a good nurse." He paused. "This fire's ready, my dear," he said, knocking down the hot coals and adjusting the vent before putting the lid on.

Sarah went into the kitchen to get the sirloin that Samuel had marinated that afternoon, and Asa asked her to bring out a bar of soap too. "I'm going to shower out back," he said. "I'm sure Isaac is taking his sweet time upstairs." He took the soap and a dry towel and kissed Sarah on the cheek.

"Go on," she said with a smile, "and hurry up. Dinner will be ready soon."

Asa stood in the shower and let the cool water drench his head and run down his sunburned shoulders and back—it felt good. He thought about the day. It seemed ages ago that he had gone running and to church. It had been another busy day, and he was worn out. When the sand had rinsed away, he peeled off his swimsuit, rinsed it, wrung it out, and hung it over the old wooden shower wall. He lathered up his hands and quickly washed his hair and then ran a bar of soap over his arms and chest. When he was almost done, he just stood there with the water beating down on his back. He looked at the white skin of his upper thighs and hips, rubbed the soap into the dark mass of curly hair, and, as he rinsed the suds away, allowed his hand to linger. He thought of the playful look in Noelle's eyes when he had asked her to come to the beach, and he recalled her teasing reply—and then he remembered how her body had felt pressed against him that afternoon. He closed his eyes and pictured her slowly unbuttoning her blouse. He imagined the smoothness of her skin and how it would feel to lightly trace his fingers along the soft curves of her breasts. Asa couldn't help himself—more than anything now, he wanted to see her alone. He put the soap on the shelf, slipped his hand back down, and leaned against the wall. He closed his eyes again and, with a slow, steady movement of his hand, felt a surge of heat course through his body with pulsating urgency.

# 10

On Tuesday, Asa was up early. He ran, showered, and was eating his second bowl of cereal when Sarah came down.

"I made your coffee," he said.

"I see that," she said, ruffling his hair. "When did you start drinking coffee?"

"Today. I thought I had better take it up since I'm heading off to college."

She peered into his cup. "Black?" she said, surprised.

"Yup, no cream or sugar for me."

"And how is it?" she asked, pouring herself a cup.

"Awful. Hey, do you think Noelle would mind if I brought Martha with me?"

"Not at all," Sarah replied. "And I'm sure Martha would love going for a ride and spending the day with you."

"All right, I will." Asa stood up and put his dishes in the sink. "What do we have for lunch?"

"There's still some leftover steak if you want to make a sandwich," Sarah replied.

"Sounds good," Asa said, opening the refrigerator and taking out what he needed.

Sarah poured herself a cup of coffee and sniffed it suspiciously.

"Hmmm . . . how many scoops did you use?"

"Four."

"Perhaps you might try a scant two next time," she said with a smile. Carrying her Bible and a cup of the strong coffee, she went out onto the porch.

Asa packed his cooler with two sandwiches, two Cokes, pickles, cookies, chips, a hard-boiled egg, an apple, and two dog biscuits. He had to rearrange his lunch twice to get the top on. He also filled a jug with ice water. He looked around the kitchen one last time to see if there was anything he had missed and decided he probably had enough. He could always stop and buy a snack if need be. Asa looked at Martha. "Well, are you finally ready?" he asked. She wagged her tail. Asa pushed open the screen door, and Martha followed him out. "I'll be home for dinner," he said, leaning down to give Sarah a kiss on the cheek.

"Okay," she said, reaching up to put her hand on his face. "Have a good day. Love you."

"Love you too."

Asa headed down the steps with Martha gingerly following along at his heels. When they reached the truck, Asa opened the passenger door. Martha looked up at the high seat and then at Asa, her sad eyes questioning.

"It's okay," he said. Martha put her front paws up on the seat, and Asa gently picked up her hindquarters and lifted her in. He tucked her tail safely beside her and kissed her head. "Love *you* too," he whispered. He unrolled her window, closed the door, and put his cooler and tools in the back, all the while, thinking about how the only girls he had ever said *I love you* to were his mother and his dog. Asa shook his head as he got in the truck. "Oh, well, ole girl, oh, well. Such is the life of a solitary man."

Asa headed out to Route 6 and turned left. As he swung right onto the rotary, Martha put her head out the window and breathed in the salty air, her wet nostrils quivering with excitement, her ears and jowls flapping as she looked at all of the cars waiting to join the circling traffic, making it obvious to everyone who saw her that she was enjoying the ride. Asa looked over and thought to himself, *Happy as a clam.* He thought of the time he had asked his father where that saying had come from. "When is a clam happy, and how do you tell that it *is* happy?" he had wondered aloud. "It certainly isn't happy when it's about to become chowder!"

His father had chuckled at the question and then asked him, "If you were a clam, you wouldn't be happy to be in my chowder?"

"No way!" he had replied. "I'd only be happy to stay in the ocean." Asa smiled at the memory as he made his way off the rotary.

They continued along Beach Road in Orleans, and Martha kept her head out the window the whole way, only pulling it in for an occasional sneeze. Finally, Asa turned onto the long driveway that led up to Nate and Noelle's house. He looked for signs of life but was disappointed to find none. He parked his truck in the shade, got out, and opened Martha's door to lift her down. She licked his nose, wagged her tail happily, and wandered off to see what interesting smells she could find. Asa put his lunch and ice water under a tree and opened the garage to get the drop cloths. He surveyed the front of the house and decided to wait on the back windows. He would work on all of them at once.

The drop cloths were heavy as he gently draped them over the shrubs to protect them from paint scrapings. He set up the stepladder, pulled off his T-shirt, turned his baseball cap around, and got to work. Asa preferred painting to scraping but was determined to do a thorough scraping job on this, one of his favorite houses. He worked diligently all through the morning and, by lunchtime, was growing weary of the monotonous work. He had devoured one of his sandwiches early in the day, but he was hungry again and decided to break when he had finished around the door.

Martha was lying in the shade next to the cooler when Asa walked over. She looked up at him. "C'mon, girl, let's go up by the pool." She slowly got to her feet and moseyed after him, her internal clock telling her that it must be time for a snack. Asa sat down at the table under the umbrella and dug into his cooler. He opened a Coke and looked around. The crystal-clear water certainly looked inviting, and he wished he had brought his suit. He would have to remember to bring it next time, along with a towel and a radio. He ate his lunch slowly and gave Martha both of her treats and one of his cookies. He filled up a little bowl he had brought with some of his ice water, and she took a drink and ate an ice cube. Asa leaned back. It was hot, even in the shade. There wasn't a single cloud in the sky. Honeybees hummed around the lilies that peered over the fence, and hummingbirds squeaked and buzzed around the bee balm. The summer air was heavy with the scent of mint and mown grass.

Asa noticed a crumpled towel on the ground next to the lounge chair on the other side of the pool. He walked over and picked it up. It was dry. He looked around again. *It certainly is private up here,* he thought. He knelt down and felt the water as a bead of perspiration trickled down the side of his cheek. *What the heck,* he decided, standing up and walking back to his chair. He kicked off his sneakers as he unzipped his shorts, looking around one last time. He quickly pulled off his shorts and boxers in one smooth motion and waded into the pool. The water was refreshing, and he dove under to cool his head. He floated around for a while, luxuriating in the freedom of no clothes. As he lay back in the water, he began to feel aroused by his own nakedness in this setting. He closed his eyes and wondered what Noelle would think if she came home right now. He opened his eyes, half hoping she would be standing there, and was disappointed when she wasn't.

Asa got out of the pool, reached for the towel, and slowly dried himself off. As he gingerly pulled his shorts up, he remarked, "Someday, Martha, we're going to make some woman very happy," and then added, "That is, if we're not leading the reclusive life—that would certainly be an obstacle." Martha thumped her tail agreeably.

"Okay, ole girl, back to work." Asa hung the towel over the chair, put his hat on, picked up his cooler and water jug, and walked toward the gate. Martha followed faithfully.

# 11

Thankfully, the afternoon seemed to pass more quickly than the morning. Asa glanced at his watch and saw that it was almost four o'clock. He wanted to be completely finished scraping before he cleaned up. As he moved the ladder again, he heard Martha barking and looked up to see her trotting toward the driveway. He watched Noelle's Bel Air pull up to the house, and his heart started pounding. Martha greeted her happily and escorted her to the front of the house. Noelle was wearing her nurse's uniform and cap, and her hair was pulled back. After a long day, though, some wisps of her hair had come loose and now fell lightly over her cheeks.

"It's a lot of work, isn't it?" she remarked sympathetically. "You must be tired." Despite herself, Noelle found her eyes drawn to Asa's torso and realized she had not seen him without a shirt in several years. He was no longer the wiry, skinny boy she had first met while caring for Annie. Instead, his chest had broadened, and his tan shoulders and arms were smooth and hard.

Asa smiled. "Yeah, but I'm making progress," he answered, looking around for his shirt.

Noelle was touched by his modesty. "I'm glad you're still here. I hate coming home to an empty house. I picked up a few things at the store. Would you like to stay for supper?"

Asa was surprised by the invitation. "I can't," he answered, obviously disappointed. "I told Mom I'd be home for supper. Thanks, though."

"Well, how about some peach cobbler, then? I still have some left."

"That sounds good," Asa replied, finally locating his shirt, turning it right-side out, and pulling it over his head. "I just want to finish this last part and clean up."

"Okay," Noelle said. "Come in when you're done." She turned to walk up the path, and Martha followed, hoping there might be a snack in the bag for her.

Half an hour later, Asa quietly pushed open the screen door and found Noelle sitting on the porch, reading a book, with Martha asleep at her feet. He glanced down at the book. It had a worn cover, and he couldn't make out the title. Hearing him come in, Noelle looked up and smiled.

"All done?"

He nodded.

She put the book down, stood, and turned to go inside. She had changed out of her uniform and looked cool and comfortable in khaki shorts and a sleeveless white blouse. Her hair was pulled up with tortoiseshell combs, and the earrings she wore matched the necklace that fell between the open buttons of her blouse. Asa picked up the book she had been reading and followed her into the kitchen.

"What would you like to drink? That's one thing I forgot to get, so I don't have much. Let's see," she said, opening the refrigerator. "Iced tea, which is almost gone, orange juice, milk, and"—she laughed—"beer. You don't drink beer, do you?"

"That sounds good," he said.

She looked up, surprised. "Are you old enough?" she teased.

"Of course!" Asa's eyes sparkled as he grinned at her.

"Hmmm," she said thoughtfully, "okay, but don't tell anyone."

"Promise."

Noelle took out two beers, set them on the counter, and started rummaging through the drawer for a bottle opener.

"I *do* know when your birthday is," she said, thinking out loud. "Give me a minute. . . . August, right?"

"Yup," Asa replied, taking the magnetic bottle opener off of the refrigerator. It was being used to post the tide chart, but he put a different magnet on the chart and opened the bottles.

Noelle heard the sound and turned from the drawer. "I always forget about that one."

Asa handed her one of the bottles. "It's when low tide is at eleven fifty-nine a.m."

"What is? Oh, your birthday! Let's see . . ." She stepped closer to him so that she could scan the chart. He looked over her shoulder. She smelled of soap, and Asa decided she must have just showered. He slipped his arms around her, and she leaned into him. "Here it is," she exclaimed. "I knew *that*—August thirty-first. How could I forget?"

"I don't know," he replied, grinning again. "After all these years, I would've thought you knew it by heart." She gently pulled away, and he leaned against the counter.

"After all these years," she said solemnly, "I *do* know it by heart, Asa. I was just teasing." She hesitated before continuing. "And after all these years, I hope *you* know how much our friendship means to me, because it's getting harder and harder for me to resist you. I'm very afraid of this path we've started down. I'm afraid of what *could* happen, and I'm afraid of the heartache it would create." She shook her head and looked away. "I don't know what to do. I keep trying to not let anything happen, . . . but when you are standing in front of me, I lose all resolve." She looked at him again. "Asa, you must be so confused . . . and I *am* so sorry."

Asa nodded slowly, his heart aching. Noelle turned away with tears in her eyes and busied herself reaching into the cabinet for the plates. Her blouse pulled out from her shorts as she stretched, and Asa couldn't help but notice the smooth brown skin of her lower back. But this time he forced himself to look away; he would do whatever she asked, no matter how much it hurt. He didn't want to think about it anymore; he just wanted everything to be the way it used to be.

He picked up the book that Noelle had been reading, determined to change the subject. Tears filled his eyes as he tried to focus on the title page, and one tear fell onto the writing before he could brush it away. It was then that Asa realized the book was an original volume of *Leaves of Grass*—and that it was signed.

"Where'd you get this?" he asked, astonished by the famous signature.

"My grandfather was a book collector," Noelle answered, thankful for Asa's simple question. "He gave it to me for my eighteenth birthday."

Asa looked at the publication date, 1855. "Gosh, it must be worth a fortune! Have you ever had it appraised?"

"No, I haven't," Noelle replied as she divided the last of the cobbler onto two plates. "I'd never sell it."

"I have the deathbed edition, but it isn't original or anything. I'm jealous!"

"Then I probably shouldn't tell you that I also have a signed *Walden*."

"You do?" Asa was incredulous. "Where did your grandfather find such treasures?"

"I'm not sure about *Walden,* but the Whitman"—Noelle

nodded to the book in Asa's hands—"he found in a dusty little shop in Cambridge."

Asa gently leafed through the pages and ran his fingers lightly over the distinctive signature before stepping out on the porch and carefully putting it back on the table. When he came into the kitchen again, Noelle handed him his cobbler.

"Thanks," he said, reaching for a fork.

Asa leaned against the counter and was lifting the fork to his mouth when Noelle said, "By the way, how is *your* poetry?"

Asa smiled. He knew that Noelle knew he wanted to be a poet—they had talked about it often enough—but still, he teased her. "What poetry?"

Noelle was at the sink, filling the glass baking dish with hot, sudsy water. She finished, turned to look at him, and said, "Asa, you keep promising that you're going to let me read some poems, but you never do."

"Well, lately, I haven't made much progress. I don't know what it is—no inspiration, no ideas. Maybe it's just not meant to be."

"Oh, I doubt that," Noelle consoled. "You're so busy with work that you probably don't have time to write. Don't be so hard on yourself."

Asa was surprised by Noelle's insight—it was almost as if she had read his mind. He took a sip of beer. "How do you like beer with your cobbler?" she asked.

He smiled. "Oh, beer's good with anything." It was quiet for a minute, and Asa looked down. The tension was palpable as they tried to retrace their steps back to the carefree inno-cence they had once shared. Finally, Asa looked up. "So, who are you taking care of now?"

Noelle let Martha lick her plate and put it in the sink. She took a sip of her beer and sighed. "Oh, you *don't* want to know," she started. "For the last year, I've been taking care of this crotchety old codger who no one else can bear," she replied. "He's ninety-two and as grouchy as can be. His family doesn't even like to visit him because he's so ornery. The good thing is he's not terminal—that is, unless you can die of a poor disposition! After David and Annie, I had to take some time off, and when I finally went back, I put in a request for no more terminal patients . . . at least, not for a while."

"Who was David?" Asa asked. He watched Noelle's eyes suddenly fill with emotion, and he wished that he hadn't asked.

"David was a young boy who had leukemia. He was as sweet as could be, and he never complained. He was very wise for his age—so insightful about life and living. Some adults aren't even able to see life the way David did—like the old codger I care for now." Noelle paused reflectively and then went on. "Unfortunately, David's mother had a very hard time dealing with his illness, and she completely withdrew from him. She left his care completely to me, and I became very at-tached—*too* attached. He was my first case, and I tried to keep from becoming emotionally involved, but it was impossible. In the end, I came to love him as much as I think I would love my own child." Noelle studied Asa. "If he had lived, I think he'd be about your age." She hesitated again. "At the time, it seemed so unfair. . . . It still does." She picked up Asa's plate and put it in the sink too. "But, Asa, God always has a plan, even though we often can't comprehend the reasons. I am just glad to have had the privilege of knowing David, even if it was only for a short time." She paused and took another sip. "How in the world did we get onto this anyway?" she asked, smiling at him.

"I asked," Asa said. Then, not knowing what else to say, he added, "I'm sorry about David."

He looked at Noelle as if seeing her for the first time. She had always been a part of his life, and yet there was so much about her that he still didn't know. Before that moment, he wouldn't have even been able to say exactly what color her eyes were. But now, as he looked, he discovered that they were the deepest blue, and behind them were secrets about living that he hadn't even begun to understand. Noelle's eyes had seen so much of life and love and death, and now those same dark eyes were looking openly at him. He ached to take her in his arms, but her plea for restraint continued to play through his mind.

"Oh, not to worry," she said, grinning. "After all . . .

> *'Great is life . . . and real and mystical . . .*
> *wherever and whoever,*
> *Great is death . . . Sure as life holds all parts together,*
> *death holds all parts together.'*"

Asa smiled and joined in.

> *" 'Sure as the stars return again*
> *after they merge in the light,*
> *death is great as life.'*"

They laughed, and it almost seemed like before. . . .

## 12

For the next two weeks, it rained on Asa's day off from working at the coast guard station. In past summers, the weather would never have kept him from visiting Noelle, but now he felt as if he needed a reason to stop by. He filled his time with reading and even did some writing, all the while wishing that the weather would cooperate so he could return to work on the house.

When the sun was shining, time passed quickly. His days were filled with morning runs, ocean swims, and working at the coast guard station. His evenings were filled with occasional outings with friends or relaxing at home with Sarah. He would never admit it, but he missed Isaac and was glad when, on Friday afternoons, Isaac and their father returned from Boston.

Isaac had settled into his own routine, too, not just one of working in the shop but also that of maintaining two relationships. Asa would just shake his head when Isaac returned to the Cape house and would immediately call Jen to make plans. He knew that Isaac was spending most of his free time in Boston with a girl named Kate.

"It's going to catch up with you," Asa warned.

"It's not like I'm married," Isaac would reply.

On Saturday morning, Samuel was making French toast when Asa returned from his run. With an empty eggshell dripping from his hand, he looked up. "Hey, I keep meaning to ask you—how's that extra project coming?"

Asa shook his head. "Well, if you mean painting Uncle Nate's house, not very well. It seems to rain every time I have a day off." He paused thoughtfully. "In fact, if it's going to be nice today, maybe I'll try to go over."

Samuel washed his hands and reached for the whisk. "Hmmm . . . I don't know if today would be good. You can check with your mother, but I'm quite sure that they are having the group over tonight, and if they're anything like us, they'll be spending the day getting ready."

Asa sat down on a stool with his ice water. "Well, at the rate I'm going, it's never going to get done."

"Maybe Isaac would be willing to stay out here one week to help you."

"I doubt it." Asa shook his head. "He's got too many extracurricular activities."

Samuel chuckled. "You're right about that." He dipped a piece of bread into the egg mixture and laid it on the hot griddle. "What about you—do *you* have any extracurricular activities?"

Asa absently wiped the moisture off the outside of his glass and thought about Noelle. He pictured her reaching for the plates and remembered how her shirt had pulled up, exposing her tan skin. Samuel looked up when his son didn't answer, and Asa just shook his head.

"Not . . . not really," he stammered.

"Well, you're welcome to stop by tonight—that's if you don't have something better going on."

"Maybe," Asa replied. "Although, I'm sure Isaac will have something better goin' on."

Samuel cut two pieces of the French toast diagonally in half and layered them on a plate. He reached into the cabinet for the sifter, sprinkled confectioner's sugar on top, and slid the plate toward Asa.

"Mmmm . . . thanks."

Asa stood to pour a cup of coffee, and Samuel looked surprised.

"Coffee?"

Just then, Sarah came into the kitchen, still dressed in her bathrobe. She reached for her favorite cup, held it out for Asa to fill, and confirmed that the gathering was indeed at Nate and Noelle's that evening.

# 13

More than anything, Asa wanted to see Noelle, but he wanted to see her *alone,* not in a crowd, so he was uncertain about stopping by.

In the end, Isaac decided for him. "Of course we'll stop by. Uncle Nate's chowder is almost as good as Dad's—and maybe we can sneak a cocktail."

That evening, after Samuel and Sarah had left for the party, Asa came inside to take a shower. On his way, he opened the refrigerator and grabbed a beer. His father wouldn't notice. He never did. Asa looked over at Martha stretched out on the cool linoleum floor. He reached into the freezer for an ice cube and slid it over to her; she chomped away happily as he opened his bottle and headed up the stairs. Isaac had already showered and was talking on the phone. Asa heard bits and pieces of the conversation but couldn't make out who was on the line. He turned on the water, took a long drink, and got undressed. Then he pulled back the shower curtain, reached for his beer bottle, and got in. He put the beer on the back shelf, let the cool water run down over his head and back, and heard Isaac come into the bathroom.

"Well, that was Kate. She wants to come out one weekend."

Asa chuckled. "Someday you'll learn!"

"Maybe . . . but for now, I just have to figure out how to keep that from happening. By the way, Jen is on her way over. She's going to drive her car down to Uncle Nate's so we can head out whenever we want."

"You mean, so you don't have to hang out with me."

"You got it."

"Thanks a lot."

"No problem—someday you'll know what it's like!"

Asa could not understand how Isaac could string along two girls. He said he loved them both, that they were different, but Asa was still not convinced that a person could truly love another—*and* be unfaithful. Then again, wasn't that what Noelle was doing? He quickly washed, dried, wrapped a towel around his waist, and went to his room. He opened his dresser drawer and looked for his faded blue polo. His drawer was full of blue shirts since Sarah loved him in blue, but the one he was looking for wasn't there. He looked in the hamper and found it. He sniffed it, and it seemed okay, but when he pulled it on, he saw there was a stain on the chest. He pulled it off again and went to his closet. There were several pressed shirts, but he picked a wrinkled white-and-blue-checked button-down. Sarah would frown, he knew, but he liked this shirt. Maybe he should iron it. . . . No, he hated ironing. He'd just tell her that the wrinkled look was in. He pulled on his shorts and finished his beer just as Jen's Corvair pulled into the driveway.

Isaac called up the stairs, and Asa headed down. His brother was out on the porch with Jen. He had helped himself to a cocktail, and Jen was sipping the clear drink from his glass. Asa saw the lime and knew it was a gin and tonic. He watched Isaac pull her close and kiss her. They both smiled and took turns sipping the drink.

"Hey, Jen," Asa said, stepping out onto the porch. He wondered why it was that he felt guilty when it was Isaac who was the betrayer.

"Hi, Asa," she said.

"Do you mind if I ride down with Jen?" Isaac asked. "I think everyone is going to the beach later." He looked questioningly at Jen.

"Yes, I think so," she replied.

"You know me," Asa sighed. "I never mind."

On the way, Asa turned on the radio in the truck and heard Roy Orbison crooning a melancholy song about the plight of the lonely. He listened briefly to the lyrics, shook his head, and finally switched to the Red Sox game. *What a great night to be at a game,* he thought. *Too bad they are having such a terrible season.* He tried to focus on the play-by-play, but as he followed Jen's car down Beach Road, he felt a growing apprehension. When they arrived, he backed into the bottom of the driveway to avoid being blocked in and walked slowly up the driveway. As he looked up at the house, his heart raced.

## 14

Noelle was standing next to Nate when they walked in, dressed simply in a sleeveless navy blue linen blouse with a low neckline and white slacks. Nate was talking to Samuel and another friend. The boys and Jen made their way over to say hello. They shook hands with the men, and then Isaac gave Noelle a kiss and introduced Jen. Asa stood back, watching the introduction. He wasn't sure if it was the color of her blouse or the shadow of the evening light, but he thought Noelle's skin looked even darker than the last time he had seen her. When she finally turned to him, he smiled but hesitated for a moment before leaning forward and kissing her lightly on the cheek. Her sandalwood perfume and the closeness of her body aroused him. Noelle pointed in the direction of the kitchen and told them she'd be right in to make sure they had found everything they needed.

The three newcomers encountered Sarah coming out of the kitchen. She looked at Asa's shirt and raised her eyebrows. Asa grinned and kept walking. Isaac ladled a bowl of chowder for Jen and one for himself, and they went out to the porch in search of drinks. Asa was fixing his own bowl of chowder when Noelle pushed open the kitchen door.

"So, how are you?" she asked.

He looked up. "I'm fine. Listen, I'm sorry I haven't been able to get back over here—"

Noelle put her hand up before he could go any further. "No apologies. The weather hasn't cooperated one bit. Is the chowder still warm?"

"Yup."

"Do you have a drink?" she asked.

"Nope." He smiled at her. "I'll have a beer, though, if there's one to be had. . . ."

"What will your parents say if they see you drinking?"

"Oh, they won't care," Asa replied, grating a little fresh pepper onto his chowder. Noelle opened the refrigerator and leaned down, reaching into the back for a cold one. Asa looked up over from what he was doing and saw Noelle's white slacks tighten around her figure. He closed his eyes and listened to the laughter and voices coming from the adjacent room. He felt a cool breeze drift through the open window, whispering across his face and rustling the curtain. For a moment, he remembered lying in bed as a boy and listening to these same comforting sounds, and he felt a sudden longing for the innocence of those days. Noelle stood and closed the refrigerator, and Asa picked up his chowder. He cradled it in one hand as Noelle handed him a plastic cup.

"I can't believe your parents won't care," she said skeptically.

"And I can't believe I'm standing in *your* kitchen—drinking again!"

"I know! *You* are going to get me in trouble," she said, relaxing into a mischievous grin.

He looked intently into her eyes. "I wish that were so. . . ."

He slowly breathed in her fragrance, suddenly not wanting to ever breathe in any other air.

"I wish it were so too," she said quietly. "If you only knew how much . . ."

Asa half smiled and reached for his cup as the kitchen door swung open.

"There you are," Nate said, coming into the kitchen with his hands full of empty bowls. He set them in the sink and rinsed his hands, filling the bowls with sudsy water at the same time. He dried his hands on a towel. "How's it going, Asa?" he asked.

"Pretty well, Uncle Nate," Asa began, "except for getting back over here. I was just apologizing to Noelle about—"

Noelle interrupted, "I told him no apology necessary. It rains every time he has a day off from the coast guard station."

"That's right, Asa, no apologies," Nate said, stepping behind Noelle and slipping his arms around her. "I'm sure it'll get done." He kissed her lightly on her neck and said, "Now, are you coming back out there?"

"Yes, I was just making sure this boy had everything he needed." She winked at him.

Asa forced a smile in return, all the while struggling to quell the surge of envy that had blindsided him as he watched their innocent, yet intimate, exchange.

"Do you need anything else?" Noelle asked.

"Nope, I'm set," Asa answered, as his heart whispered, *Actually, there is—quite a bit more . . .*

"Okay, well, let me know if you think of anything," she said as she followed Nate out of the kitchen.

Asa just nodded. After they had gone, he leaned against the counter, took a sip of his beer, and breathed deeply. Noelle's scent lingered, teasing his senses, and he closed his eyes and imagined that she was still standing there. . . .

## 15

After putting his bowl in the sink and refilling his cup, Asa wandered out to the pool. He walked along the edge of the yard and suddenly remembered the path to the beach that he and Isaac had worn through the scraggly growth when they were younger. He wondered if it was still passable. He looked back at the pool to get his bearings and then walked about ten feet to the left. There it was, a bit overgrown but still visible. He pushed aside a branch and remembered the way as if it were only yesterday that he and Isaac had chased each other, defying the gnarled undergrowth scratching their bare skin and tumbling out to the waves. Tonight, as he drew closer to the thundering surf, he could almost hear Isaac shouting, *Last one in is a rotten egg!*

Asa reached the opening to the beach and slid down the dune, catching his shirt. He slipped off his L.L. Bean camp mocs, shook out the sand, and walked to the water's edge. The moon was hazy, but Asa could make out the turbulence of the waves. He stood there, silently watching and trying to understand the tempest that was stirring inside of him. After a while, he finished his beer and walked back to the place where the path opened up. He set down his shoes, put his cup in one of the shoes, and turned back to the ocean. He had no desire to return to the party. He walked along the water's edge and listened to the waves. His mind was full of questions. He knew that what had happened with Noelle was wrong, but in his heart it had felt so very right. *How could that be?*

Long ago, Asa had sat out on the porch with Sarah while she was reading her Bible. He had tried to explain to her the way that he prayed. He told her that he liked to "think to God." He said it was more like sharing his thoughts than praying. Sarah had smiled at his description. She pictured God smiling, too, when He was included in Asa's thoughts. She imagined that God treasured her young son's simple and honest faith.

Now Asa naturally did what he had always done—he turned his thoughts into a prayer, knowing that God was listening. *As much as I tout living the simple life, I do want to fall in love and be loved. How else can I be a poet? I know there is no way for anything more to happen with Noelle, but, damn— sorry—I just can't stop thinking about her. No doubt I am attracted to her—she is beautiful—but she is so much more than that. She is funny and easy to talk to and she likes poetry. Why is it that the one woman I fall for is taken? And even though I know this can never happen, I let myself think about her. I am such a fool!*

As Asa continued along, he noticed a family walking slowly ahead of him. A young couple, holding hands and laughing, was followed by a pair of footprints that wandered carelessly along the beach. Ahead of the couple, two small figures darted back and forth, chasing the waves and stooping to pick up stones and shells. The two figures often ran to the couple and dropped their treasures into the pail that the man was carrying, and then they raced off again in search of more treasure.

Asa suddenly realized that he was looking at his own life. *Did You put this family in my path to remind me of my own childhood? To remind me of all of my parents' efforts to teach and guide me? Could You have known that I would walk this stretch of beach on this night and struggle with these feelings?* Asa had been raised to believe that there were no coincidences in life, but he was still amazed when moments like this occurred. Moments of grace, Sarah called them. *Perfect timing*, he thought. He smiled and stopped. He didn't want to intrude on the family's walk. Asa watched them disappear into the night and then turned back. Walking along on the edge of creation, he believed and trusted that he was the singular focus of God's attention. *Thank you for listening. I guess I'll just have to keep busy and focus on finishing Nate's house, keeping my head on straight, and then focusing on school. Perhaps, though, if You have time, You might keep an eye out for a girl like Noelle . . . for me. . . .*

Asa reached down to pick up his cup. As he stood, he glanced at his watch. He had no idea it had gotten so late. He slipped on his shoes, climbed up the dune, and carefully made his way back through the brush. He silently stood in the yard and looked up at the house. The party had ended. The house was dark except for the forgotten Christmas lights that twinkled on the back porch. There was a light on in an upstairs bedroom too.

For some reason, standing in the dark and looking up at the window, Asa thought of Annie. The light blinked out, and Asa walked slowly down to his truck, thankful that he had parked away from the house.

## 16

Noelle finished the last of the dishes as Nate dried and put them away. So often, simple tasks like this reminded him of Annie. She had always filled the sink with hot sudsy water, so the bowls would still have some bubbles on them when she put them in the dish drain. Noelle, on the other hand, allowed the hot water to run so she could give each plate a good rinse. Nate also remembered how diligent Annie had been about keeping the bird feeder filled and how much she had enjoyed watching her little troupe of chickadees, nuthatch, titmice, and wood-peckers. The cardinals, though, had been her favorite, and she had often looked out the window at dusk and said, "Mr. and Mrs. C are here for their bedtime snack."

Noelle loved the birds, too, but the feeder sometimes hung empty and forgotten. Nate would look out and say, "Mr. C is tapping his foot, waiting for his breakfast."

And Noelle would look out and laugh. "Well, you'd better go out and give it to him!"

Nate missed Annie deeply and found it disquieting when, in the darkness of their bedroom, he caught himself thinking of her while making love to Noelle. He knew it was unfair, and it made him feel guilty and confused. Nate loved Noelle, but he still loved Annie—he always would.

As Noelle slipped into bed, she reached up to turn off the bedside light.

"Leave it on," Nate said.

"Why?" she asked, feigning innocence.

"Just because . . ."

"Didn't your mother ever tell you that 'just because' isn't a reason?" she teased.

"Mmmm," Nate murmured, pulling her close. "But she forgot to tell me to watch out for the quiet ones."

"I bet she did," Noelle whispered huskily as Nate's tongue lightly danced on her bare skin.

"I just want to be able to see all of you."

"Why? Are you afraid you'll forget who I am?" she teased.

At these words, Nate hesitated ever so briefly. It was barely a pause, but it was enough. Noelle's heart stopped as she looked down at his face. Nate's eyes were closed, unrevealing, and he did not reply. Noelle didn't move or say anything more. She just lay there and allowed him to explore her body.

"I love you so very much," he finally murmured, easing himself onto her and kissing her softly.

Noelle closed her eyes and, for the first time, did not try to shut out the thoughts of Asa that continually teased her mind. When Nate moved to her side again, she reached up to turn off the light and lay facing the wall. Nate slipped his arm around her waist and fell asleep, and as Noelle listened to the waves and to the slow, even sound of Nate's breathing, a tear trickled silently down her cheek. In the darkness of the room full of memories, she knew that she would never be the only one he loved. She lay awake, and somewhere in the distance, she heard a truck start.

# 17

Sarah was waiting when Asa came in. He looked at his watch. It was 11:55. He grinned. "Made it," he said. "Sorry to have kept you up, though."

"Well, I'm just glad you're home. Where were you? We saw your truck when we were leaving and thought you must have gone with Isaac, but he said he hadn't seen you."

"Oh, I just went for a walk on the beach, and I guess I lost track of time."

"By yourself?"

"Yup."

"Well, I'm glad you're home and safe," she said. "Don't forget about church," she added as she headed up the stairs.

"Me? Forget about church? Never!" he teased.

"You don't need to be fresh."

"Okay . . . sorry. Good night, Mom. Love you."

"Love you too. Good night."

Asa sat down on the floor on the edge of Martha's bed. She looked up at him and put her head contentedly on his lap as he stroked her velvety ears. She closed her eyes and sighed. Asa leaned back against the wall and thought about the childhood memories that had slipped into his mind that evening. Against a backdrop of blurred time, these memories were still as clear as if they had just happened. It amazed him how a simple sound or scent could trigger the memory of a moment or feeling. *The ability to remember is so amazing,* he thought. *It's as if certain memories have something more to tell, something more to teach, and that is why they are remembered so clearly.*

In the morning, Sarah came down early and found Asa asleep next to Martha, his arm draped over her side, her head tucked neatly under his chin. She recalled how often she had found Asa, when he was little, sleeping on Martha's bed. It had been years, however, and the sight of her grown son asleep on the dog's bed brought a smile to her face and tears to her eyes. Martha looked up. Except for her thumping tail, she didn't dare move.

## ❧ 18 ❧

The following Tuesday, Asa skipped his morning run. A heat wave was in the forecast for the Cape and the Islands, and he wanted to get an early start. He filled his jug with ice water and packed an empty water dish for Martha. He wondered if he should leave her home on such a hot day, but when he saw the longing in her eyes, he relented. "Make sure to find a shady spot," he warned. She wagged her tail, and he helped her into the truck.

Fifteen minutes later, Asa pulled into the hardware store. Martha leaned out the window. "Be right back," he called. He bought the paint, Antique Barn Red, and two brushes. He came out, put them in the truck, and walked quickly to the deli next door. He noticed how warm it was already and noted that he wouldn't be able to leave Martha in the truck at all later. He ordered two sandwiches for lunch and poured a black coffee while he waited. He also bought a quart bottle of Tropicana. He went out to the truck, loaded his cooler, and climbed in. "Good girl," he said, gently pushing Martha over to the passenger side. She wagged her tail and resumed her position as copilot with her head hanging out of the red '53 pickup.

When he pulled up to the house, Asa saw the turquoise Bel Air parked in the driveway, and his heart raced. However, he was determinedly resolved to stick to his plan. He parked the truck, helped Martha out, and put his cooler in the shade. As he walked toward the garage to get the drop cloths and ladder, he noticed the water hose was snaking up over the stone wall and into the backyard. As he walked up the path, he saw Noelle giving Martha a drink from the hose.

She looked up and smiled. "Well, good morning! I was just innocently watering my garden when this big black beast came bounding up behind me!"

"Sorry. Did she startle you?"

"Only a little."

"I didn't expect you to be home today. Is it okay that I brought her?"

"Oh, it's fine. She's such a sweet old girl," Noelle said, rubbing Martha's head. "Anyway, I'm home because one of the other nurses needed to switch days this week. I wasn't sure if you'd be coming, but I thought if you did, I could help you paint."

This unexpected turn of events caught Asa off guard. He faltered but regained his composure enough to answer, "I'm sure you don't want to spend your day off painting in the hot sun. It's supposed to be miserable today."

"Well, I don't want to cramp your style, but I'm happy to help."

Asa didn't know what to say. Finally, he managed, "Well, if you're sure it's what you want to do."

"I'm sure—I just have to change."

Asa was stirring the paint when Noelle returned with Martha at her heels. She had on a pair of worn tan shorts and one of Nate's old white V-neck T-shirts. Looking up, Asa decided that Noelle would look beautiful no matter what she was wearing. *This isn't helping,* he thought. At the same time, he wondered how he was going to get through the day.

The morning flew by, and Asa found that he had never enjoyed painting so much. He had dragged a second stepladder from the basement, and they had started out at opposite ends of the house.

At the outset, Asa had teasingly challenged, "Bet I can beat you to the front door."

"You're on!" Noelle had replied, laughing. "But if you get any red paint on my blue hydrangeas, you automatically lose."

The trim around the windows had always been painted the same shade of red as the clapboard, so the job was simple. They worked steadily all morning, and an easy conversation ensued. Asa found himself often stopping to watch Noelle paint and to listen to her tell stories. It was a comfortable feeling, almost like old times.

Over the course of the morning, Asa learned that Noelle's father had been a Baptist minister and that her mother had spent her life "serving others." Noelle and her older brother Pete had been raised in a home where the needs of others were always put first, even when their own needs were barely being met. However, Noelle recalled that there always seemed to be just enough. She laughed and said, "Every meal was like the loaves and fishes. No matter how many sat around our supper table each night, there was always plenty. And my mother was such a good cook that we often had folks stop in who didn't really need a meal. It just smelled so good outside that they found a reason to knock!"

Asa laughed at this, his own stomach rumbling at the mention of food. "So, you were a preacher's kid?"

"Yup," she laughed. She hadn't heard the term in a long time.

The two worked quietly for a while, and Asa tried to picture Noelle as a young girl sitting in an old white New England church. He saw her head solemnly bowed in prayer, her hair in pigtails. He pictured her giggling in the front pew just like any other preacher's kid who thinks they own the place. He smiled and wondered how well she knew her Bible.

He looked over, cleared his throat, and started reciting, "Genesis, Exodus, Leviticus, Numbers, Deuteronomy, Joshua, Judges, Ruth, First and Second Samuel, First and Second Kings, First and Second Chronicles . . ." But then he faltered.

Noelle looked up, smiling, and picked it up. "Surely you remember Ezra, Nehemiah, Esther, and Job . . ."

"Of course I do. Psalms, Proverbs . . ." Asa stopped again, grinning.

Noelle easily recited the rest of the books in the Old Testament, and Asa laughed. "Oh, well, I used to know them." Noelle paused and then started in on the New Testament.

Asa held up his hand, "All right, all right, you win. You don't need to show off!"

They went back to painting, Asa still trying to picture a younger Noelle. There was so much that he didn't know about her, and he suddenly wanted to know *everything*. He wondered if her parents still lived in Maine. He decided to ask, and when Noelle told him that they had both passed away when she was in nurse's training, he wished he hadn't. Asa said he was sorry, and Noelle assured him that it was long ago and that they had lived full lives. She went on to say that after her mother died, her father, despite his deeply religious background, had been a lost soul and had died less than a year later—on their wedding anniversary. Asa tried to imagine the love—and loss—Noelle's father must have felt to die of a broken heart.

Asa's stomach had been rumbling for an hour when Noelle finally offered to make sandwiches.

"I brought lunch," Asa said. "In fact, I have two, if you'd like one."

"I'm sure you brought two because you can eat two."

"Actually, I skipped my run this morning, so I really don't need to eat both of them. You're welcome to have one."

"Okay."

"Do you want to have lunch up by the pool?"

"Sounds good. I'm just going to get some iced tea. Want some?"

Asa pulled the bottle of orange juice out of his cooler. "I'm set," he said. "Thanks anyway."

"You certainly come prepared."

Martha followed Asa up to the pool, and Noelle joined them a few minutes later. She was carrying a large glass of sweet tea and a plate of chocolate chip cookies. "These cookies are not holding up very well in this heat. You'd better eat them."

Asa looked at the melting chocolate. "Oh, we won't have any trouble with those, will we, Martha?" Martha wagged her tail agreeably, happy to have her name mentioned in close proximity to the word *cookies*. Asa handed Noelle one of his sandwiches and leaned back in his chair in the shade of the umbrella. Noelle took half and wrapped the other half back up.

The air was heavy with the monotonous trilling of crickets and the hum of laboring bees. *The unmistakable sounds of a steamy July day, sounds reminiscent of simpler times,* Asa thought, absently composing. *The wings of the season, droning endlessly, blissfully ignorant of summer's fleeting hours . . .*

They sat in a comfortable silence for a while, eating their sandwiches. A bluebird alighted on the wooden gate and burst into a song. "Look!" Noelle whispered. Suddenly, his mate called from the tree line, and the flash of cobalt was off again, as quickly as he had come.

Noelle finished her sandwich and reached for her iced tea. "Did you bring your suit?" she asked.

"No, but I meant to. I meant to bring a radio too."

"Well, you can borrow a pair of Nate's shorts if you want to jump in."

Asa looked at Noelle and said slyly, "I didn't need shorts the other day."

Noelle feigned shock. "You mean you went skinny-dipping in *my* pool?"

Asa reached for the uneaten half sandwich, smiling. "Well, it was just *so* damn hot, and I didn't want you to come home and find me suffering from heat stroke. I really *was* just thinking of you." He couldn't help but look in her eyes as he said this.

"Well, at least you were thinking of me," she teased.

"Always," he said with a smile.

"So, what's stopping you today? I can go paint, and you can cool off."

"Or . . . you could join me . . ."

"Mmmm . . . that would be fun. But as enticing as it sounds . . ." Noelle smiled gently. "I'd better not. *You* still could, though."

"No, that's all right," he said. "You're just saying that so you'll finish your half of the house before me." He grinned at her as he finished his drink.

She laughed. "You know, Asa, you'll never be able to conceal where you're from with that accent."

Asa broke a cookie in half and gave it to Martha. "You're one to talk," he teased, standing up.

Noelle laughed, knowing it was true.

# 19

The front of the house was sunnier in the afternoon, making the job almost intolerable. Martha had found cool shade under a nearby tree, and Asa envied her, wishing he could take off his shirt. He and Noelle worked in silence for a while.

"If you want to quit, it's okay by me," he said.

"You just want to win."

"I didn't realize you were so competitive," he teased.

"Well, when you grow up in the shadow of a big brother, it's kind of a survival thing."

Asa laughed. "I know what you mean. By the way, what does your brother do now?"

Noelle looked over at him and gave him a half-smile. "Asa, you're going to think it's not safe to be around me."

Asa looked puzzled, then realized what she was going to tell him. He shook his head. "I should just stop asking questions."

"That's okay. I don't mind. When Pete and I were growing up, our lives were influenced by our parents' examples of service to others. It was only natural for Pete to enlist. My father was torn by Pete's decision. On one hand, as a man of God, he didn't believe in one man taking another's life. At the same time, however, he was so very proud of his son. My mother was heartbroken when he shipped out, and when we received the news that he had been killed, we were devastated. Everyone loved Pete. I was only sixteen at the time, but seeing my parents' heartache, I can honestly say that it shook their faith to the core."

Noelle paused and then went on. "Asa, Pete died doing what he was raised to do: help others. For me, looking back at the course of his life, I realize now that it had always been leading up to that moment. Like so many other brave men, he gave his life for others. In time, my parents grew to realize this, too, but the initial shock was almost more than they could bear."

"You have certainly seen more than your share of tragedy," Asa said quietly.

"Mmmm." Noelle was then silent and lost in thought. Soon she smiled again. "Enough about me! How 'bout you?"

"Oh, there's not much to tell," Asa said, shaking his head. He had finished painting around the second window and was closing in on the door frame. "It's been my strategy to distract you, though, so I can win."

Noelle laughed. "And you say I'm competitive?"

"Didn't I tell you this morning? Last one finished buys the beer."

"Is that so?" Noelle dipped her brush and began painting with renewed vigor.

An hour later, Asa stepped back and viewed the house. Noelle put down her brush and stood beside him. She reached up and lightly put one hand on his shoulder and leaned against him. He knew it was an innocent gesture, but to Asa, the touch of her hand rushed through his body like a brush fire burning through dry tinder.

"Looks good!" she said.

Asa nodded slowly, not wanting to move—afraid to move—

afraid that she would take her hand away. And now, the only thing he wanted was to feel her touch.

Noelle gently squeezed his shoulder and laughed. "Well, I guess the beer's on me!" Then she added, "Pizza, too, if you'd like . . ." She stepped away and grinned at him. Asa smiled back. He looked at the tan of her flushed cheeks. He studied her dark eyes and the way her hair, damp with perspiration, fell across her forehead. He wanted to reach out and gently touch her face, to lightly brush her hair back into place. Instead he held his arms stiffly at his sides and struggled to gain control over his desire.

*God, please help me. I don't know if I can keep doing this.*

## ❧ 20 ❧

After Asa left to pick up the pizza, Noelle replenished Martha's water and hurried upstairs for a shower. She washed quickly, wanting to be back downstairs before he returned. She was toweling dry when she glimpsed her reflection in the long mirror hanging on the back of the bathroom door. She paused and slowly ran her hand over the flatness of her tan stomach and she stood up straighter. *Not bad for thirty-two,* she thought. She looked at the fullness of her breasts and then turned slightly to see her backside. *I could still pass for twenty-five . . . maybe . . . Well, okay, twenty-six.* She sighed. *Eighteen is long gone, though.* She studied her body. *What am I thinking? This is crazy!* She threw the towel at the mirror and pulled on a pair of clean white shorts and a pink sleeveless blouse. As she brushed her hair, she pictured Asa's blue eyes and the crooked way his mouth curved up on one side when he laughed. *He is definitely a cute kid,* she thought, *but that's the operative word:* kid—one who, *I'm sure, already has plenty of female attention!*

Hearing the truck in the driveway, Noelle hurried downstairs. She was just opening the fridge when he came in. "Hey, that's not fair," he said, seeing that she had showered and changed.

"Well, you can shower, too, if you'd like."

Asa quickly considered the opportunity to stand in the shower where Noelle had just stood—*naked.* The invitation was tempting.

"No, I'm just kidding," he heard himself say, and then added, "But I was thinking—would you like to walk down to the beach with all this?"

"*Walk* down?"

"It's not far—there's a path behind the pool." Noelle looked puzzled. How could she not know that there was a path from her own yard? "Isaac and I wore it in years ago. It's a little overgrown, but it's still passable."

Twenty minutes later, Asa had laid out a beach blanket and was trying to tune in a small portable radio. The crowd on the beach was thinning out, but some late-day sun lovers still lingered. Noelle sat down on the blanket and opened the pizza box. She recognized the lyrics of a Patti Page hit from three summers earlier. "I love that song. Can you get it to come in?"

Asa slowly turned the knob, and the lyrics lilted sweetly into the evening air. Noelle sang along softly to the famous song about loving old Cape Cod. Asa just listened and sipped his icy beer. It tasted good after the long, hot day. The song ended, and as Asa reached for a slice of pizza, the announcer said, *"Now here's another summer song for all you lovers out there, from last year's hit movie starring Sandra Dee and Troy Donahue. See if you recognize this one."* A popular instrumental theme drifted from the radio, and Noelle asked Asa if he had seen the movie. He nodded as he hungrily devoured his first slice before Noelle even started.

They sat quietly, looking out at the waves, and Asa began to notice the silence. Noelle reached for a slice of pizza. "Now, back to what we were talking about before."

Asa looked questioningly at her over his beer bottle.

"Don't you remember?"

He shook his head.

"You."

"I already told you—there isn't anything to tell. Nothing new or exciting, and besides, you already know everything."

"I'm sure I don't know *everything*. After all, here you are, Asa, on the cusp of life, full of hopes and dreams and heading off to college—that's very exciting."

"Well, it should be, but sometimes I think I would rather just stay here and get a job and never leave the Cape. I love it here." He paused before continuing. "Going to college will definitely be different from going to prep school. Isaac had already been at the Gunnery for a year when I started. He was always around, and that made it easy for me. By the time he graduated, I was very comfortable being there." He shook his head. "This won't be the same. I'm not like Isaac."

"Well, I'm sure you'll do fine. Colleges take great strides to make sure their freshmen become oriented and settled. Besides, you will be so busy with classes, making friends—and meeting women—you won't have time to be homesick."

Asa looked over at Noelle and raised his eyebrows. "Meeting women? I'm afraid I'm not very good at that. Besides, not only are there *no* women at Dartmouth"—he hesitated and caught her eye—"but I'm already hooked on *someone*."

"Oh, Asa." She smiled gently at him. "If I were ten years younger *and* not married," she added with a frown, "you would be just the kind of guy I'd be looking for—funny, handsome, not to mention poetic. I could go on, but I don't want it to go to your head!"

Asa shook his head again. "Noelle, I don't think there will ever be another . . . like you."

"There will be, Asa," she said softly. "I promise."

Asa looked out at the waves, and his mind drifted. He

thought back to the day last fall when he had gone hiking with a group of friends at school. The October air had been crisp and cool. Flames of color had swept the countryside and shimmered against the sapphire sky. Lane, a local girl, and two of her friends had come along and had brought a couple bottles of wine. They had walked along the Shepaug River and hiked up to the pinnacle. There they had lingered on the rock outcropping, reveling in the radiance of the late-afternoon sun and passing around the wine.

Later, still feeling euphoric, they had ventured into an abandoned train tunnel. Asa had just walked into the darkness of the turn inside the tunnel when Lane had slipped her hand into his and pulled him back. He had looked at her questioningly and had suddenly felt her warm lips, tasting sweetly of wine, pressing softly against his. He had been so surprised that he had just stood there. Even so, he had been thrilled by this turn of events and had held her hand until they had reached the trailhead. After that day, though, Lane had seemed embarrassed and avoided him. Asa decided that it was his weak response to her kiss that was to blame.

Noelle watched Asa wipe the condensation on the outside of his bottle and wondered what he was thinking.

"Well, enough about me," he said, genuinely unaware that he *hadn't* actually spoken but had only *thought* about that day. "I bet you were a handful as a teenager," he said, turning to Noelle.

"Me?" She laughed. "I was an angel, of course!"

Asa opened a second beer for himself and one for Noelle. "Here," he said, handing it to her. "There's truth in wine."

She laughed. "It won't help, remember? I was a P.K."

"That's the worst kind," he teased.

"Well, I suppose you're right—maybe I wasn't perfect."

Asa laughed. "You see, there *is* truth in wine!"

"I haven't even had any yet."

"Well, go ahead, and then tell me how you *weren't* perfect."

Noelle took a long drink and thought for a moment. *Is this really something I should be talking about?* "All right," she began. "There was, perhaps, one time when I wasn't exactly an angel." She studied Asa. "But I was young, and at the time, it just felt right. It was the summer after Pete shipped out. His best friend Tom had just turned eighteen and couldn't wait to catch up with him. I had had a crush on Tom for years. He was tall and slender, and all the girls thought he was dreamy. After Pete left, Tom continued to come by our house to talk and to find out if we had heard from Pete. I could tell that he missed him, and I honestly thought that was the reason he was coming by. I was so innocent—I certainly didn't think he was coming to see me.

"Anyway, the night before he was to leave, our church had a reception for him. At the end of the evening, we were having a hymn-sing around the campfire, so Tom and I ran up to the choir loft to grab some hymnals. . . ." Noelle paused and took a sip of her beer, she seemed lost in her thoughts. Asa watched her but didn't say anything. The only sounds were the pounding surf and the wistful lyrics of the Platters coming from the radio.

Noelle smiled. "This station always plays such good songs. They bring back so many memories." Asa just nodded. "Anyway, where was I? Oh, yes, the hymn-sing. Well, the sanctuary was dark—especially in the choir loft—and I tripped and dropped my hymnals. Tom knelt down to help me, and then everything happened so quickly. He had tears in his eyes, and he told me he was afraid of not coming back, afraid he would never get married, never make love, and I . . . well . . . I . . ." She paused, then smiled mischievously at him. "I guess I'll have to leave the rest up to your imagination. . . ."

Asa watched her, his whole body aching. He had never

known desire like this. "Sixteen and . . . and in a church?" he stammered in disbelief. "I guess you *were* a little wild!"

"Hey, now, I like to think of it as a sort of 'last request'!"

"Well, I guess that's one way of looking at it," Asa replied. They were quiet, and Asa started to visualize Noelle at sixteen, lying on her back in a dark choir loft. It was more than he wanted to think about, so he stopped himself. "Do I dare ask what happened to him? Please don't tell me he died too."

Noelle half smiled and shook her head. "We wrote back and forth during his tour, and I saw him once when he returned. He came to visit Pete's grave, and I went with him. But after that, his family moved away, and we lost touch. The war had changed him, and I guess it just wasn't meant to be.

"But, Asa, please . . . all this is just between you and me. I don't know how you get me to talk so much. Even Nate doesn't know about this. . . ."

"Don't worry," Asa replied. "Your secrets are safe with me." He leaned back on the blanket and looked up at the stars. Frank Sinatra was softly crooning an old Gershwin song. Asa listened in wonder to the words that he had heard so many times growing up, words that now seemed to be meant just for him. *Oh, how he needed someone to watch over him. . . .*

## ≈ 21 ≈

In the days that followed, Asa could think of nothing else. He slept fitfully and had almost no appetite. He declined invitations to go out with friends, and to Sarah he seemed sullen and brooding. It was not until she had asked him several times what was troubling him that Asa realized that he needed to do a better job of concealing the madness that was churning inside. Sarah, for her part, hoped that her son was just anxious about school and prayed that his uncharacteristic mood swings would simply subside. By Friday morning, her prayers seemed to be answered. Asa appeared, smiling, at breakfast, kissed her lightly on his way out, and whistled a carefree tune as he walked to his truck.

By Friday afternoon, however, his heart was once again full of an increasing, familiar apprehension. He pulled slowly up the sandy driveway to the old red Cape and looked up at the massive stone chimney protruding stoically from the center of its roofline. He pictured the mason that had stood high above the ground almost two hundred years earlier, toiling under the same hot sun and looking out in awe at the same rugged coastline. He imagined the intensity of the man's concentration and the sweat dripping from his brow as he carefully chose each stone for the most impressive part of the chimney.

To Asa's dismay, Noelle wasn't home yet. He parked the truck, lifted his toolbox out from the bed, and walked around to the back porch. He opened the door and called out a hello just to be sure. It felt strange to walk into the empty house, almost as if he were an intruder. He headed up the stairs, his heart pounding. The bedroom door was open, and he walked quickly across the room, set down his toolbox, and pushed the window all the way up. He took out the screen and set it against the dresser just as Nate had done. As he turned back to the window, the bed caught his eye. It was neatly made with the quilt pulled tightly to the headboard, but Asa did not see the quilt. Instead, in his mind's eye, he saw only a snowy white sheet strewn quickly aside. He stared at the middle of the bed and saw Noelle lying naked, her arms stretched freely above her head. He saw Nate next to her, his fingers gently running along her abdomen and slipping down between her thighs, teasing her. Asa squeezed his eyes shut and shook his head. *This is crazy. I am crazy!*

He reached for his toolbox and climbed out onto the roof of the porch. A cool breeze swept across his hot cheeks, clearing his mind. He forced himself to study the sill and the casing around the window. He knew that the window had pulleys and weights just like those in the coast guard station. The job was a bit tricky. He would need to carefully pry the outside casings off, as well as the blind stop, and expose the side jamb. The side jamb would then need to be pried away from the sill in order to free it enough to cut the nails off with a hacksaw. Only then would Asa be able to remove the sill and fit the window with a new one. He set to work, concentrating on the task at hand and shutting his mind to the room beyond the window.

He worked steadily, prying the dry wood of the side jambs

carefully so that they did not split. He had just cut the visible nails and was trying to free the sill when the pry bar suddenly slipped and tore into the palm of his hand. Asa shouted out in surprise and pain. He immediately knew that the cut was deep. He grabbed the shirt that he had taken off and wrapped it tightly around his hand and climbed in the window. As he rummaged through a drawer in the bathroom cabinet for a bandage, he heard a voice on the stairs.

"Asa?"

His heart skipped a beat. "Up here," he replied, still looking for a bandage.

"Are you okay?" Noelle asked, reaching the top of the stairs. Asa straightened up, and when Noelle peered in the door, he had his hand behind his back and was grinning sheepishly. She looked at him suspiciously. "What did you do? Let me see."

"It's nothing."

"If it's nothing, why are you hiding it?"

Asa slowly held out his shirt-wrapped hand.

"Oh, Asa. How bad is it?"

"I don't know. . . . I'm afraid to look."

Noelle reached over and gently unwound the T-shirt from his hand. The last layer of fabric had a good-size red stain on it as she gingerly lifted it away. In the center of his palm was an angry gash about an inch long.

Noelle's nursing instincts immediately took over, and she pulled Asa to the sink and thoroughly washed the wound. Asa grimaced as the water rushed over the cut.

"When did you last have a tetanus shot?" she asked.

"Last summer—when I stepped on a nail."

"That's good, and this has bled quite a bit, which is also good. Bleeding flushes out bacteria." She turned to the medicine cabinet and took out a tube of Bacitracin ointment and then turned to the linen closet for gauze and tape. Asa leaned against the bathroom counter and felt self-conscious without a shirt to put on. Noelle expertly bandaged his hand, talking the whole time. "It will probably throb tonight, and you will have to keep it clean. You must be very careful to not let it become infected."

Asa just nodded, watching Noelle and wondering at his good fortune. *Could accidentally stabbing my hand be lucky? If it meant being cared for by this beautiful nurse, then yes, definitely! I would do it again in a heartbeat!*

Noelle neatly finished wrapping his hand and then leaned down to pick up the shirt. She turned to the sink and ran it under cold water, rubbing the fabric together. "How does it feel?" she asked, not looking up.

"Fine . . . thanks," he replied, still watching her.

Noelle rang out the shirt. "This stain should come out. I have a load of wash to do if you'd like me to throw it in too." She glanced up at Asa, and for the first time noticed his bare chest. Asa's curly light hair was not nearly as thick as Nate's, but it caught the light of the late-afternoon sun and shone against his smooth brown skin. "In the meantime, you can borrow one of Nate's," she added, looking quickly away and setting the wet shirt on the counter. Asa stood in the bedroom doorway as Noelle opened Nate's top drawer, pulled out a freshly laundered shirt, and threw it to him.

"Thanks," he said. He could feel his pulse throbbing through every vein of his body as he searched Noelle's eyes for any sign of encouragement. *Just a smile, a nod, or better still, take my hand . . .* Asa tried desperately to will Noelle's next move. More than anything, he wanted to take her in his arms and hold her. Standing alone in the bedroom, the opportunity seemed so perfect, so fleeting. Noelle glanced at the bed, and Asa's heart stopped. Then she quickly turned and looked at the open window.

"Do you need help with your tools?" she asked.

"What?" he said with uncertainty.

"If you bring them in, I'll put the screen back."

"Oh, right." He pulled on the T-shirt and climbed out onto the roof to gather his tools. "I just need to measure this sill so I can pick up a new one." He quickly measured, jotted down the measurement, threw everything in the toolbox, and climbed back in. He watched Noelle fit the screen into the window, and his heart plummeted when she brushed past him, retrieved his wet shirt, and immediately headed down the stairs. He leaned against the door and stared at the bed.

Alone in the kitchen, Noelle opened the refrigerator and closed her eyes. She felt the cool air on her face and tried not to think, but her mind was flooding with thoughts of Asa. *It would be so easy to love him.* She took out two bottles, opened them, and prayed, *Oh, God, please help me. I don't know if I can stop this. It already feels so out of control.*

Asa came into the kitchen, and Noelle turned and handed him a frosty bottle. "It's the least I can do," she said with a half-smile.

"Actually, there might be more," he said quietly.

"Asa . . . ," Noelle started.

But he interrupted her and tried to look innocent. "What I mean is . . ." He faltered. "Is there any more peach cobbler?"

Noelle laughed, relieved by the question. "I'm all out, sorry, but I was wondering if you'd want to stay for supper. I have hamburgers, and I made macaroni salad last night."

Asa hesitated. "All right," he answered. "That sounds good."

"Great. Just let me run up and change."

Asa wandered out to the porch and leaned back in one of the chairs. He tried not to visualize Noelle changing, but it was impossible. He nursed his beer and felt his hand begin to throb. He closed his eyes and resolved to simply be content to be *here*—there was nowhere else he would rather be.

In a few minutes, Noelle returned and Asa opened his eyes. She had retrieved her bottle from the kitchen and sat down across from him.

"So, how did that happen anyway?" she asked.

"I don't know . . . I was being careful. I'm glad it's my right hand, though."

"That's right—you're a southpaw, aren't you?"

He nodded.

"Well, at least it won't affect your writing." Noelle took a sip.

"Mmmm . . ."

"Have you *been* writing?"

"Some."

"Hey, I thought you were going to share."

Asa grinned and absently wiped the condensation on the side of his bottle. "Did I say that?"

"Well, I thought you were . . ." Just then, they heard steps on the walk, and Nate pushed open the screen door. He had his suit coat over his arm and his tie loosened from his neck.

"Well, well, is this a private party?" he asked with raised eyebrows and a tired smile.

Noelle was the first to speak. "Not at all," she replied, standing and greeting him with a kiss. Asa stood as well but looked away at their exchange. Nate turned to Asa and reached out to shake hands. Asa held up his bandaged hand and smiled.

"Uh-oh, what did you do? I hope that didn't happen here."

Noelle looked at Asa and answered for him. "I'm afraid it did."

Nate shook his head. "I'm sorry, Asa. How bad is it?"

"Not too bad," Asa said, feeling the throbbing in his forearm now.

"He did agree to stay for some nourishment, though—" Noelle began.

"Actually," Asa interrupted, "I think I'll take a rain check. I'm beat. Thank you for the invite, though . . ."

Noelle looked surprised. "Are you sure?"

"Yup." He smiled at her. "I'm sure." He went into the kitchen, finished the last of his beer, and put the bottle in the sink. He came back out, reached down for his tools, and turned to Nate. "I'll pick up the new sill tomorrow and come by to put it in."

"Don't worry about that," Nate said. "Wait and see how you feel."

"It's nothing. I'm fine." He turned to Noelle. "See you."

"Not if I see you first," she said with a grin.

Asa turned to go, and Nate watched him.

After the truck was gone, Nate stood behind Noelle and put his arms around her. She leaned into him and closed her eyes. They stood quietly, taking each other in. Finally Nate said, "You do realize, don't you, that *that* boy is in love with you?"

Noelle's heart stopped as she tried to feign surprise. "Asa?"

"Don't tell me you don't see the way he looks at you?"

"I don't," she insisted, avoiding his eyes. "And *you* are being silly!"

"Well, you'd better be careful not to hurt his feelings. You don't know what it's like to be a vulnerable teenage boy."

"That may be true," she said, feeling stung by his words. "But believe it or not, I *do* know what it's like to be a vulnerable teenage *girl*."

"I can't say that I blame him," he whispered, turning her to him and kissing her lightly on her neck and cheek before slowly finding her lips.

# 22

When Asa arrived home, Isaac was walking toward Jen's car with a cooler in one hand. Seeing Asa, he smiled broadly. "You're just in time! We are going up to P-Town to see the sights. Want to come along?"

"Nah, I don't think so," Asa said, climbing out of the truck. "I did a job on my hand, and it's throbbing." He knew the misery he felt was much more than physical, but the excuse would satisfy his brother.

"Oh, c'mon," Isaac went on. "We've got a cooler full of your favorites. They will surely ease the pain."

Asa looked in the cooler and hedged a bit. "Hmmm . . . Do I have time for a quick shower?"

"A *quick* one," Isaac replied with a smirk. "Not one of those long ones you like to take."

Asa punched his brother with his good hand and headed inside.

It was tricky taking a shower while trying to keep one hand dry, but he managed. Soon he was in the back of Jen's car with a cooler between his feet and a cold one between his legs. He had decided that he could ease his pain and drown his sorrow all at the same time. The wind blew his damp hair as he took a long drink, looked out the open window at the sultry summer sky, and imagined Noelle again—as he had that afternoon—lying in bed beside Nate. His mood would have been infinitely darker had he known, at that very moment, the image *wasn't* only in his mind.

Jen's car had been a high school graduation gift from her parents, and Isaac loved to drive it. The sporty little Corvair Monza headed up Route 6, and the party began. Asa had never been one to drink to excess. Tonight, though, he didn't care. He wanted to forget everything and feel nothing. Isaac watched his brother in the rearview mirror with a mixture of interest and concern, but by the time they reached Provincetown, Asa was feeling fine. Isaac parked the Corvair on a side street, and they walked toward downtown.

Growing up, Isaac and Asa had been to Provincetown only a handful of times with their parents. When they were too young to notice the town's culture, Sarah and Samuel had taken them along and wandered through the art galleries and shops. But as the boys got older, Sarah found it simpler to avoid exposing her young sons to the flamboyant community than to try to explain a lifestyle that she had trouble understanding herself. Now, Asa and Isaac loved to trek up to P-Town with friends, especially at night. They loved the crazy bohemian atmosphere, the wild parties that spilled out onto the streets, and the colorful outfits and personalities of the town's residents.

Tonight, as the three wandered down Commercial Street, Asa became much more animated. He put his arm around Jen's shoulder. "Jen," he began, "did you know that Eugene O'Neill walked down this *very* street?"

Jen laughed. "Yes, Asa. You told me last time. You also told me that E. E. Cummings lived here."

"Well, did I ever mention Harry Kemp?"

"No, who was Harry Kemp?"

"Who *is* Harry Kemp?" Asa corrected with exaggerated disbelief. "Why, he is only the Poet of the Dunes!" Asa exclaimed. "He still lives nearby in a shack made of driftwood that his friends built him for his birthday."

"That sounds comfortable," Isaac teased. "Now I know what to get you for your birthday."

"Did he write anything I might recognize?" Jen asked.

Asa stopped walking and thought for a moment. Then he raised his hand solemnly. "'The poor man is not he who is without a cent, but he who is without a dream.'"

Jen nodded slowly. "That sounds familiar," she said, winking at Isaac.

Asa, not noticing, continued on. "I have heard he hasn't been well, though—"

Isaac interrupted, "Jen, look at this old structure. It used to be a stable for the horses that drew carts up from the harbor, carrying oysters."

"Right here in town?"

"Yup."

"Jen," Asa interjected, "do you know what they call such a building in Britain?"

"No . . . but you're going to tell me, aren't you?"

"It's a mews," Isaac said, stealing the answer from his brother.

"Well," Jen teased, "you two are just a wealth of trivial information!"

"Yup," Asa agreed. "It comes from having a storyteller for a father."

Jen looped her arms through the arms of the two boys and, laughing, steered them into one of the many taverns that lined the wharf. They found a table out on the deck overlooking the bay, a perfect spot to watch the sun sink into the horizon. Isaac ordered a round of drinks and a large platter of steamers.

Asa was enjoying his alcohol-induced respite from the obsession that plagued his mind. He liked watching Jen playfully tease his brother and silently wished for a simple relationship like theirs. Then he remembered that Isaac had someone else, too, and he felt sad for Jen. Asa was just finishing his beer when the waitress came over with a tray of drinks. "The gentleman at the bar sent these over," she said.

"Uh-oh, Jen," Asa started to tease.

At the same moment, they all looked over and saw a man leaning against the bar, alone. He was good-looking, very tan with short, salt-and-pepper hair and rimless glasses. He was wearing light shorts, a black shirt, and sandals. He turned to them and smiled directly at Asa, who quickly looked away, his own smile fading into embarrassed astonishment.

"Uh-oh, Asaaa," Jen said, trying to stifle a giggle.

"Uh . . . Asa?" Isaac looked at him questioningly. "Is there something we should know?"

"Oh, right, I've been holding out on you." Asa's cheeks flushed.

"Well, you never know—maybe that gentleman sees something in you that you have failed to acknowledge. You do, after all, have that artsy, poetic side," Isaac teased.

Asa, however, was not amused. "Let's go," he growled.

"What? And waste these fresh free ones? Get off it, Asa. You know I'm just teasing."

Asa sat back silently and waited for Jen and Isaac to finish their drinks. He would not touch the one that was meant for him, and he avoided looking over at the bar. His normally good-natured disposition, influenced by alcohol, embarrassment, and frustration, had darkened dramatically. Nothing they said could cheer him. Finally, he excused himself and said he would be waiting outside.

Asa walked along the dock and peered down into the dark water. As if to confirm his own sexuality, he allowed his mind to relive the moment when he had stood with Noelle in the bedroom that afternoon. This time, though, she reached for his hand and pulled him toward her. He felt her press against him and knew she could feel how aroused he was. . . .

"Asa," Isaac called from the dock. "I don't know what's with you lately." He shook his head. "Anyway, we're heading out."

# 23

Year-round residents of the famous Massachusetts peninsula enjoy the relatively moderate climate of their corner of New England. However, that is not to say that they don't have their share of storms. In autumn, an occasional tempest of the sea actually does follow the weatherman's prediction and make landfall. And in winter, classic nor'easters do occasionally hug the coast and bury the sand with snow. For the most part, though, Cape Codders are not forced to face the endless snowfall and harsh temperatures that their northern neighbors endure. Likewise, when southern New England is suffering through a stretch of heat and humidity, Cape Cod is usually enjoying an ocean breeze and significantly cooler temperatures.

When Asa was finally able to return to the house in Orleans, the Cape had already seen two days of unusually oppressive heat and humidity. A promise of relief was forecast, but only at the expense of severe thunderstorms, and Asa was anxious to replace the sill before it rained. He headed over after work, and with great apprehension, pulled up the sandy driveway. He was relieved and at the same time disappointed to find no one home. *Well, which is it?* he thought to himself. *Relief or disappointment? How can it be both?*

He grabbed the primed sill, his toolbox, and his shoulder bag from the front seat. He had brought his notebook along, although he wasn't sure why.

He climbed out onto the porch roof and looked toward the sea. The sky was already an ominous gray. He set to work fitting the sill into the frame. When he had nailed it in place, he still had to rig the knotted end of both ropes into the grooves on the inside of the window. He patiently lifted the window, slid the knots into place, and pulled the window down. The window, offset by the weights, glided easily in its tracks. Asa gathered up his tools just as the wind began to whip at his clothes. He climbed inside, and with the curtains billowing around him, replaced the screen and gently closed the window. Asa then went to the other bedrooms and closed all of the windows. In the guestroom, he recognized the ornately carved bed frame that had been Annie's. He was suddenly ashamed of his feelings. *What would Annie think of all this?* He shook his head, as if trying to dislodge the errant thoughts and clear his mind once and for all. He heard a distant roll of thunder and turned to go down the narrow stairs.

# 24

Asa was putting his tools in his truck when Noelle pulled up the driveway. She smiled and waved as she rolled up her windows.

"Hi, how's your hand?" she asked as she got out.

"Better, thanks."

"Are you just getting here?" she asked, reaching into the front seat for a shopping bag.

"No, I'm all done and heading home."

Noelle looked disappointed. "Oh," she said, glancing at the sky. "I certainly hope this storm breaks this humidity." As if on cue, the wind picked up again. "Hey, by the way, did you hear that Harry Kemp died last week?"

Asa looked surprised. "Gosh, no. I hadn't heard. I knew he wasn't well. . . . We were just talking about him."

"I think it happened last Tuesday."

Asa shook his head in disbelief. "Oh, well . . ." He paused. "Anyway, your bedroom window is all set, and I closed the other upstairs windows, but I forgot to check the downstairs."

"Okay. Thanks." She paused. "Listen, would you like to stay—"

Asa shook his head. "I would, but I really should get going." He could not have felt more torn, so he just stood there, wishing that some greater force would intervene. A sudden clap of thunder split the sky above them, and large raindrops splattered on their arms and faces. "You better go check those windows," he said, opening the door of the truck, rolling up his window partway, and climbing in.

"Are you sure you won't stay? I made a peach cobbler."

"That's tempting," he said with a grin. "But I'm sure." He had never been more uncertain of anything in his life. Noelle stepped back and smiled as Asa waved. He looked in his rearview mirror and watched her running into the house. He pulled away as it started to pour and couldn't believe he had the will to leave. It was only when he reached the end of the driveway that he remembered he had left his shoulder bag on the porch.

# ❦ 25 ❧

Asa almost slipped as he ran back up the wet stone walk. The wind was whipping the trees in the yard, and he glanced over and saw movement by the pool. Noelle was struggling to close the patio umbrella before the wind took it away along with the glass tabletop it protected. With head bent, Asa ran to give her a hand, and then laughing, they raced for the house.

"Why'd you come back?" Noelle sputtered, trying to catch her breath.

"I forgot something." He looked at the raindrops running down her cheeks and smiled. Then, unable to stop himself, he looked down at her blouse and teased, "Looks like you got a little wet."

"Oh, and you didn't," she laughed. "Would you like a towel?"

"There's no point—I'm just going to get wet again."

"What did you forget anyway?"

Asa nodded toward the shoulder bag by the door.

Noelle raised her eyebrows. Asa tried to act nonchalant as he reached for it, but Noelle was closer and picked it up first.

The top was open, though, and as Noelle swung it in front of her, Asa was able to reach in and slip out the notebook.

Noelle's eyes lit up. "Is that some of your writing?"

Asa laughed. "Might be."

"Did you bring it for me to read?"

"Maybe . . . ," he teased, taking a step back.

"Don't tease—I *really* am interested."

Asa stepped back again until he was leaning against the frame of the kitchen door. He slipped the worn book behind his back. He still wasn't sure if he was ready for anyone to read his thoughts—especially this woman, who would surely figure out *what* had inspired them.

Noelle didn't step forward. "Asa, I only want to read them if you're ready to let me."

Asa studied her dark eyes, searching again for the answer that only she knew. *I am ready to let you,* he thought.

"You can read them," he said finally, but his smile was gone.

Noelle took a step toward him with her hands by her sides, not reaching. She just stood in front of him, and Asa's heart pounded. He drank in the clean scent of her body mixed with the fresh fragrance of summer rain. Noelle did not look away but held the gaze of the clear blue innocent eyes that longed to know so much more. . . .

# ❧ 26 ❧

All around them and within, the storm persisted. Noelle leaned toward Asa and brushed her lips against his skin. She tasted the nape of his neck and breathed in his sweet boy-man scent, her heart pounding in disbelief. Then she searched for his lips, his warm mouth, his gentle kiss in return.

"What do you want?" she whispered.

The boy could not answer. Aching desire, as ancient as time itself, consumed him. His mind, his heart, his innocence swayed from balance. Finally, the man he didn't yet know looked into her questioning eyes, and his answer was barely audible.

With hands still at her sides, Noelle pressed her slender body against him. She realized how aroused he was and immediately felt a tingling warmth between her legs. She slipped her hands under his shirt, and the book fell from Asa's hands. He slowly pulled his damp shirt over his head and leaned back against the wall. He watched in stunned silence as she slowly undressed in front of him. Her body was tan, and he pictured her lying naked by the pool. She smiled gently as she reached for the button of his shorts. He looked down and watched her knowing hands unbuttoning, unzipping, touching him, teasing him. He wanted to touch her, too, but he was afraid to move, afraid that somehow the moment would end. He watched as she teased herself with his body, and he could barely hold on. She slowly guided him, and finally, trembling, he pulled her closer and pushed himself deeper. All at once he was amazed and confused and frightened by their intimate act. As a boy listening to stories of pirates and shipwrecks, he had innocently fallen asleep on this porch. Now, on a steamy summer afternoon years later, his boyhood was no more—and the peace of innocence would never be his again. Instead, he found intimacy and passion and jealousy for which he wanted no forgiveness.

## ❧ 27 ❧

Afternoon became evening. The storm passed, and the sky gave way to the last rays of the late-summer sun. Hours earlier, Asa had followed Noelle up the narrow stairs to the quiet bedroom whose silent walls already knew so many secrets. He lay beside her, and she watched his face while she played with his body. He searched her eyes and pulled her closer. He wanted to explore, tease, taste every part of her—and she let him. As the shadows in the room grew longer and played upon the walls, Asa learned the intimate secrets his body had longed to know.

At last, in the evening darkness, he gently eased himself off and lay beside her. He leaned over to softly kiss her, only to discover that her cheeks were wet with tears. The amazing happiness he felt was immediately shattered by fear. He leaned up on his elbow. "Why are you crying?" he whispered.

"Oh, Asa, I don't know what I've gotten us into. . . ."

"What do you mean, what *you've* gotten us into? You didn't do it alone."

"I should have known better. You are so sweet and so easy to love."

"No, *you* are so easy to love. I have never felt this way before."

"I know, but what do we do now...with what we've begun?"

"I don't know..." He paused. "Are you ready to go again?" She laughed. "Hey, at least you're laughing!" Asa's stomach growled as he said this.

"Are you hungry?" she said, smiling.

"Well, a long time ago, someone promised me some peach cobbler."

"And did you like it?" she teased.

"If that was peach cobbler, I want some more," he said, kissing her neck and playfully rolling back on top of her. She laughed, and his stomach growled again.

"I think you need some *real* sustenance."

"Oh, you're all the sustenance I need," he said, burying his face in her neck until she giggled.

"Hey! That tickles...and besides, I'm a little hungry too."

"Well, in that case, I guess we can go have a little something."

Asa rolled over and felt around for his shorts. Noelle turned on the light beside the bed, and Asa watched her. He was still astonished that this beautiful, unclothed woman had been lying beside him. He watched her look for something to put on. He saw her reach for a man's shirt, and his heart stopped. She must have had the same thought because she quickly put it down and found a robe instead.

# 28

In the kitchen, Noelle turned on the stove light and opened the refrigerator. Without asking, she took out two beers and began rummaging around in the drawer for the opener. Smiling, Asa took the magnetic bottle opener off the freezer door and opened one of the bottles.

Noelle heard the sound and looked over. "I absolutely never remember that one." She smiled. "And that reminds me—God, you're not even old enough."

"Well," he began slowly as he stepped toward her, "you have to admit"—he reached out and pressed the icy bottle against her exposed skin—"I'm pretty mature for my age."

Noelle tried to push the bottle away, but he pulled her closer so it was pressed between them. She laughed and he kissed her.

"Mmmm," she murmured, "you *are* definitely mature."

Asa backed away, grinning, leaving her holding the bottle.

"Hey, I make pretty mean scrambled eggs," he said, changing the subject. "Are you interested?"

"Sure," she said, surprised by the offer.

Asa opened the other beer, took a sip, opened the refrigerator, and took out eggs, butter, cheese, and milk. Noelle took out a frying pan, plates, utensils, and a bowl and then switched on the kitchen radio. Billie Holiday was singing the old Cole Porter classic "Let's Do It, Let's Fall in Love." Noelle smiled and started singing along to the line about Cape Cod clams "doing it."

Asa smiled and felt as if he had found his dearest friend.

They ate eggs and peach cobbler at the table in the corner of the porch with only the Christmas lights and a candle for light. A warm summer breeze drifted in off the ocean, but the oppressive humidity of the last few days was gone. They talked easily about other things, both clinging to the magic of what they had found, neither ready to face the tragic reality of what they had lost.

## 29

After the kitchen was cleaned up, Asa called home and told Sarah that his truck was stuck in a sand dune near Race Point. Sarah said she would come right out and pick him up, but he convinced her that he would be fine; he would just sleep in the truck and have it pulled out in the morning. After some back-and-forth, she reluctantly agreed. Asa hung up with a sad, sinking feeling. He had never lied to his mother before.

Noelle looked up from Asa's notebook when he stepped out onto the porch. "These are wonderful," she exclaimed.

Asa sat down next to her and looked to see which one she was reading. He didn't say anything.

She noticed the serious look on his face. "Should you get going?"

"No, I told her the truck was stuck."

"Oh." She paused. "I wish you hadn't. . . ."

"Well . . . it's done."

They sat quietly together, yet, at the same time distantly apart, each realizing that eventually—somehow—they would both have to look into the eyes of loved ones . . . alone.

After a while, Noelle turned back to the notebook, and Asa watched her read. "These really are amazing," she said. Finally, she closed the book and looked at him in wonder. "*You* are a very talented poet!" She smiled and added, "And someday *I'll* be able to say 'I knew you when!'"

Asa laughed and teased, "You could also say you knew me *when* . . . in more ways than one."

Noelle slipped her leg over Asa's lap, and he put his hands on her hips and pulled her onto him. She studied his no-longer-innocent eyes and whispered, "Yes, I could even say I knew you intimately. . . ."

"Mmmm," he replied, "perhaps you'd like to know me intimately again, just to be sure . . ."

"Mmmm, I probably should—you know, just to be sure."

## ❧ 30 ❧

Asa stood by the window. The moon illuminated the tide's incessant attempts to cling to the shore, only to be repeatedly forced to relinquish its grasp. Every so often, he saw a faint beam of light passing across the waves. He turned from the window and watched Noelle as she slept. He was still amazed that this woman had told him she loved him, had lain beside him, had made love to him. He slipped back between the sheets beside her, and somewhere, in the recesses of consciousness, realized with profound sadness that this night could never be lived again.

Noelle turned to him in her sleep and reached for his hand. Asa slipped his hand into hers and, closing his eyes, longed for time to slow down. All he ever wanted now was to taste, smell, touch, fully absorb every new sense again, sadly realizing that each incredible moment, once lived, would instantly become just a memory.

As all these thoughts swirled in Asa's mind, he had no way of knowing how often the memory of this night would haunt him—how often in the years to come he would ache with the intense longing to live it again.

## 31

Sarah decided that she must have misunderstood. She had already walked along the water's edge for at least an hour, carrying a plate of supper that had grown cold. She tried to remember exactly what he had said until, reluctantly, she finally turned back. Returning home, she didn't sleep well, frequently waking with a start and picturing Asa alone trying to sleep in an uncomfortable truck. She woke early, made coffee, and was already sitting on the back porch with her Bible when the sun peeked over the horizon. She watched it creep upward into the dawn sky. It was only moments before the bright orange streak became a fully visible sphere. No other time during the day, she thought, was the rotation of Earth and the passage of time more evident. She turned to her Bible and tried to read. She hated it when she couldn't concentrate. She set the book aside and closed her eyes. *Forgive me,* she thought. *I'm just worried about Asa. He seems so different lately. I wish I knew what was bothering him. I wish I knew where he was last night.* She sat there for a long time until she finally heard the familiar sound of Asa's old truck laboring on the grade. *Thank you,* she whispered.

Asa trudged up the stairs and was startled to see Sarah sitting on the porch. He didn't know why he was surprised—it *was* her spot first thing in the morning. He just wasn't prepared to try to be himself so suddenly. He needed time to figure things out. *Who was he now?* His mind raced. *A liar? A traitor? Someone who could betray his parents . . . and their dearest friend?*

Just moments ago, he had kissed Noelle and held her, never wanting to let go. When he finally did, he felt as if part of him were tearing away, his soul grieving for the time already past. The memory of the last twelve hours continued to burn through him, including the last hour when Noelle quietly told him that Nate would return that afternoon and stay for the last week of summer. Intense flames of jealousy had seared through his entire being, consuming him with a fury of emotions.

In facing Sarah, however, Asa was forced to stand straight, deny this inner turmoil, and act as if nothing at all had happened to him. Tears burned at the edges of his eyes as he forced a smile.

"Hi," Sarah began. "How'd you sleep?"

"Okay," Asa said, scratching Martha's head. "That old truck is far from comfortable."

"Tell me again where you were stuck?"

Asa vaguely repeated the area of the beach near Race Point, and Sarah nodded thoughtfully. She realized with certainty that she *hadn't* misunderstood.

"Who pulled you out?"

Asa's mind raced. He had never lied to Sarah before, and now it was just one lie after another. *Who could he say that his mother would not know?* "N-nobody," he stuttered. "I finally got it out using some driftwood." *That sounds so lame,* he thought.

Sarah just nodded. "Well, I'm glad you're home, safe and sound. You must be hungry."

Asa wasn't hungry at all, but he seized the opportunity to head inside and escape more questions—questions that could only be answered with more lies. He went into the kitchen and poured a cup of coffee. He had grown to like the taste, now with a little cream. He opened the refrigerator and immediately saw a covered plate of food. His stomach tightened. *Was that just left over from last night, or had Mom brought it up to the beach for me?* Asa leaned back against the counter and shut his eyes. He thought again of the night before and convinced himself that it was just his guilty conscience. Anyway, he didn't care. He didn't care if it was wrong. He didn't care if he burned in hell; the devil could have him—as long as *he* could have this woman who had said she loved him. . . .

# 32

After Asa left, Noelle sat on the stone steps with tears streaming down her cheeks. *What have I done?* She sat in the warm sun and shook uncontrollably. *Is it possible to love two people? Is it love that I feel for Asa, or does he fill some lost longing? It happened so quickly. It felt so right. Now that he's gone, though, it just feels wrong—so very, very wrong.* Over and over, the words echoed in her mind. *Oh, God, what have I done? How will I face Nate? How will I make love with him? Surely he will know.* Through a blur of tears and remorse, Noelle stared at the empty bird feeder and tried to justify her actions. A cardinal came to the feeder but, finding it empty, flew away. Slowly, Noelle tried to pull herself together. *Nate must never know. Asa said that my secrets were safe with him, but that hadn't included this. God, he is just a boy—a boy with his whole future ahead of him. What right have I to do this to him?* She remembered the look in his eyes, the sweet longing. *I do love him, but this must never happen again. I will explain it to him, he will have to understand.*

Resolutely, Noelle stood and dried her eyes. She took the

bird feeder down and filled it. She went into the house, made coffee, and went upstairs. She reached into the linen closet for a towel and glanced over at the white sheets strewn about the bed. Tears burned her eyes again, but she squeezed them back and got undressed. Seeing her reflection in the mirror, she hesitated. *This is what he saw.* She ran her fingers across her breasts. *This is what he touched.* She ran her fingers down . . . *God, I still want him.*

## ❧ 33 ❧

Asa let the water wash the soap away. The thought had crossed his mind to never shower again, but he knew that was impossible. He closed his eyes and pictured Noelle lying beside him. He remembered the way it looked to push himself deep inside her, and he ached to have her again. He thought about what it would be like to shower together. *Maybe next time.* Then he realized he didn't even know when next time would be. He slipped his hand down and tried to remember every detail of the night before as he leaned back, the water beating over him. *God, I want her so much. . . .*

## 34

When Nate came home that afternoon, Noelle was on her hands and knees, washing the kitchen floor. She glanced up quickly and forced a smile.

"Don't come in here. The floor's wet."

"I see that," he said, leaning against the doorjamb. "When you're done, though, you're going to have to wash the sheets again."

Noelle's heart stopped. "Why's that?" she asked without looking up.

"Because you must have filled the bird feeder before you hung them out to dry," he said, laughing. "Now the birds have left you their calling card."

Noelle's heart started to beat again. "They didn't!" She tried to sound annoyed. She had decided that the less she said, the better—at least until she felt reassured that Nate didn't know something had happened. *Deny it*, she told herself. *Stare it down. The shadows of guilt will make you crazy if you're not strong. Always deny. This sickening nausea will pass—it must pass. Think of other things.* She wrung out the rag and backed farther across the floor. She knew that she must act normally, but she didn't know what normal was anymore, so she would just keep busy.

"We're having steak if you want to start the charcoal," she said without looking up.

"Sounds good. Hey, did Asa finish the window?"

"Yes," she said, his name ringing through her. "It's not painted, though."

"Well, now that I'm off, I can finish painting it. He has done enough."

Noelle didn't answer.

# 35

After his shower, Asa packed his cooler, told Sarah he would definitely be home for supper, kissed Martha on the head, and headed for the coast guard station. It was his last day of work. He couldn't believe how quickly the summer had flown by. At the beginning of their summer break, he and Isaac had agreed to take the last full week of August off to relax and just go to the beach. Now Asa regretted it; every remaining day was fleeting and too precious to spend with his brother.

All day, he thought of nothing else. He needed to talk to Noelle, to be alone with her, to arrange to meet somewhere—*anywhere*. Working under the hot sun, he began to think that maybe he had only dreamed the events of the night before. He needed reassurance, he needed to know she was okay, to hear her say that nothing had changed. His mind began to race with an endless stream of tragic scenarios. He pictured Noelle confessing to Nate and promising to never see him again; he pictured her eyes full of pain and anger, telling him it was all a mistake, telling him to never come back. Tears burned at Asa's eyes, and he brushed them away. Why was he doing this to himself? None of that had happened. He shook his head and tried to think of something else.

Isaac and Samuel returned from Boston early in the afternoon, and by the time Asa got home, Isaac had made plans for the weekend. Asa tried to excuse himself, but Isaac would have none of it. Finally, Asa decided that maybe it would be good to get his mind off things.

Isaac had rounded up the usual crowd. The itinerary for that night included a game they had made up two summers earlier. It was called Shot Mini-golf, and the rules were simple: Any golfer in the party who did not make par on any given hole had to drink a shot—discreetly, of course. If a player chose to take a mulligan, they also had to drink a shot. Mulligans were popular with everyone, and usually by the eighteenth hole, no one ever made par. Finally, if someone managed to get a hole in one on the last hole, a new bottle was produced and they played again. In the history of the game, Isaac had managed two hole in ones on the eighteenth hole, and when they woke the following morning, no one forgave him. Asa survived this Friday night without drinking any extra shots. And he had a good time, even though Isaac called him a wet blanket. Asa didn't care because, by the end of the workday, he remembered that he still needed to finish painting the window and had devised a plan to pick up a small can of paint and stop by the house. This plan gave him renewed hope, and he didn't want to be hungover.

## ⊰ 36 ⊱

Noelle didn't sleep well. She lay quietly next to Nate as hot tears trickled down the sides of her face and dripped onto the curve of her ears. She wiped them away, eased to her side, and tried not to wake him, fearing that he would reach for her, and she just couldn't bear it—not yet. Finally, she pulled a robe around her, went downstairs, and sat in the darkness on the porch. She thought of Asa and wondered how he was managing. And she wondered again why she had let it happen. Finally, she dozed off and didn't wake until the first rays peeked over the dunes. She made coffee and showered. When she came back down, Nate was scrambling eggs.

"We need eggs," he said. "I used the last four."

"Okay," she answered. "I'll add them to my list."

"Seems like you just got eggs."

"I had eggs a couple times this week, and I made a cobbler," she replied, pouring two cups of coffee.

"I see that. I'm glad you left some for me," he replied teasingly, eyeing the small piece that was left. "Hey, Sam mentioned that they're combining the last Gin and Chowder with

Asa's birthday. Do you have any ideas of what we could get for him?"

Noelle's heart skipped a beat. "I don't know . . . I'll have to think about it."

Nate looked over her shoulder at the sports page. "Damn, I forgot the Sox had a twi-night doubleheader against Baltimore tonight. That would've been fun." He scooped the eggs onto two plates, buttered the toast, and set the plates on the table. "Hope you're hungry."

## 37

Asa was up early. He had not gone running in days, and it felt good to run hard. The prospect of seeing Noelle that afternoon propelled him forward. On and on he ran. He noticed a woman sitting in front of the Fo'c'sle when he passed and wondered who she was. She smiled and waved, and Asa waved back. On his return, Asa looked up at Nauset Light and imagined how the bluff must have looked when the Three Sisters had stood guard.

After a shower, Asa wolfed down some of his father's blueberry pancakes, grabbed his hat, said something about painting, and was out the door before either parent could ask a question. He stopped at the hardware store, apprehensive about what lay ahead, anxious for the inevitable first moment to be over. After making his purchase, he got back in the truck, glanced at the quart of paint, and, without knowing why, took his hat off and dropped it on top of the can.

Nate was just getting ready to run some errands when he heard Asa's footsteps. He pushed open the screen door.

"Well, look who's here," Nate said, smiling and holding the

door open with one hand while reaching out to shake Asa's hand with the other. Asa still had a bandage on his palm, and he winced slightly at Nate's firm handshake. "We were just talking about you."

"You were?" Asa asked with alarm.

Just then, Noelle appeared in the doorway and smiled warmly. "Yes, we were. We've been trying to figure out how much to pay you for all the work you've done."

"Oh, well, I've been thinking. . . . You really don't need to pay me—"

"Nonsense!" Nate interrupted. "You've earned it. And besides, what would your father say if I didn't pay you? All he talks about now is managing those two tuitions. Asa, did you happen to keep track of your time?"

"Well, I think it was about thirty-five hours in all, but I was hoping to finish painting the window today."

"Fine . . . fine . . . thirty-five, and don't worry about the window. I'm taking a few days off now, so I can finish it up. In fact, I was just heading out to get the paint."

Asa stood there, his mind racing. The only words he heard were *heading out.* He glanced at Noelle. She was leaning against the door frame with her arms folded. She was barefoot and had on a sleeveless turquoise blouse, unbuttoned at the neck, and a white skirt. She felt his eyes undressing her and looked away.

Asa thought about the can of paint in the truck and started to speak. "I already have . . . I mean . . . I already *planned* on finishing the window today—that is, if you'd like," he stammered.

"Well, if your heart is set on it," Nate said. He looked at Noelle questioningly. "So, the bank, eggs, and the hardware store?"

"You don't have to get eggs. I have a few other things to pick up later."

"Well, what are they? I can get them."

Noelle went into the kitchen to get her list. Asa stood, watching and silently calculating the length of time Nate would be gone.

Nate took the list and looked at it. "Well, my dear," he sighed, "if Asa wants to paint, maybe I should just go to the bank and the hardware store. I don't want to tie up his whole day."

Asa's heart sank as he cut the calculated time in half and wondered why he had insisted on painting.

Nate felt for his wallet, pushed open the screen door, eyed Asa, and said, "That last piece of peach cobbler is mine."

Asa nodded.

# ❧ 38 ❧

They listened to the tires on the driveway, and Asa turned to Noelle.

"I've missed you," he said quietly, pulling her toward him.

"I've missed you too." She felt his arms around her and began to lose her resolve. He brushed his lips against her cheek, slowly making his way down the curve of her neck before searching out the soft lips he remembered so well. She closed her eyes and let him. "Oh, God, if you only knew how much I want you," she murmured.

"Well, how quick can you be?" he teased, sliding his hands under her skirt and pressing himself against her.

Noelle felt how aroused he was already and knew she was losing control. *I cannot let this happen again!* Finally, she put her hands on his chest and pushed him gently away.

"Asa, I can't do this." She stepped back, still holding his hands. "I can't do this to Nate—and I can't do it to *you*. I am so very sorry to have initiated it. I don't know what else to do. You know I love Nate." She reached up and put her hand on his cheek. "And, Asa, I love you too," she whispered. She looked into Asa's sweet summer eyes, which were full of sorrow, and her eyes filled with tears. "I'm so sorry."

Asa's eyes stung, and he squeezed them shut. He pulled his hands out from hers and wiped his eyes with his palms. He turned away to look out at the ocean. He couldn't look at her, the pain and confusion were unbearable. His joy was plummeting, his hope and desire were crushed by despair and jealousy.

Noelle stood beside him and put her hand on his shoulder. "Asa, I will never forget the amazing night we had—it meant so much to me." She paused. "Listen, someday you will meet some lucky girl, and she will mean the world to you, and you will forget all about me." Asa's shoulders sagged as the tears he could no longer control spilled down his cheeks.

Finally, he turned to Noelle. "I won't feel this way again," he said quietly. "And I will never forget about *you*. Don't you see? You are the only one I will ever want—the only one I will ever love, like this."

Noelle could not bear to look into the eyes of this boy whose heart she was breaking. She looked at the tears on his cheeks and gently wiped them away. He closed his eyes and felt the loveliness of her fingers on his face.

"What will become of us?" she murmured. She lightly traced his lips, and Asa opened his mouth to taste her touch.

Outside in the morning sun, the songbirds fluttered back and forth between the bird feeder and the brush that lined their small sanctuary. The finches scolded each other and dropped more seeds than they ate. The juncos were thankful for the finches' bad manners, and the chickadees called cheerfully to each other. Presiding over the entire troupe, Mr. Cardinal perched high up in the oak tree and sang a song of contentment.

# 39

There was a line at the hardware store that busy Saturday morning. It seemed as if everyone was planning to finish up their summerhouse projects that weekend. Nate waited patiently in line, chatting with a neighbor.

"Hey, Nate, what can I get you?" Jack, the owner, asked.

"I need a quart of that antique red we use, and I'd like to square up my bill."

Jack nodded and went to mix the can of paint. He came back with the can and the list of charges made that summer. "Did you already go through the other can?" he asked.

Nate looked puzzled. "What other can?"

"Sam Coleman's boy was in here this morning, picked up a can and charged it to your account. Hasn't he been doing some work for you?"

"That's funny . . . I just saw him, and he didn't mention it." Nate shrugged. "Guess he forgot. Anyway, he's done a fine job if you're ever looking for someone to do some work."

"I'll keep him in mind."

Nate paid his bill and headed out the door.

# ❦ 40 ❧

Asa and Noelle did not hear Nate's car pull up. They did not hear the door slam shut. The only warning they had was the sudden, startling sound of wings as the mourning doves and songbirds flew to safety.

When Nate came in, Asa was at the sink filling a glass with water and Noelle had rushed up the stairs. Asa's heart was pounding, and his cheeks were flushed.

Nate glanced at the peach cobbler and nodded. "Guess I better eat that pretty soon," he commented with a grin. He handed Asa the can of paint and a new brush. "By the way, did you happen to buy paint this morning?"

Asa felt like he had been caught red-handed. "Oh, I did . . . I completely forgot. I'm sorry . . . I'll give you the money for it."

"Don't be silly. It's always good to have some around for touch-ups."

"All right . . . I'm sorry about that." Asa grinned sheepishly, amazed that he was capable of so many lies.

He took the paint and brush upstairs and knocked gently on

the bedroom door. He listened, but Noelle didn't answer, so he slowly pushed the door open. "Noelle, may I come in?"

She was standing by the window, looking out at the ocean. The screen door downstairs banged shut.

She turned to him. "Asa, this is crazy," she said in a hushed voice. "Do you realize what *almost* happened? If Nate ever finds out, he will be devastated. You *must* promise me you will never say anything—to anyone."

Through the end window, Asa could see Nate out by the pool. He looked steadily at Noelle. "I promise . . ." Then he half smiled. "It *was* fun, though." He pulled his shirt over his head, let it drop to the floor, and knew she was looking at him. He turned to take the screen out of the window. "Do you know where that drop cloth ended up?" When he turned back to her, she was holding it in her hands. He took it from her, threw it over to the window, reached for her hand, and pulled her on top of him onto the bed. She laughed. "*You* are crazy, you know—and completely unsatisfiable!"

He rolled her over so that he lay on top, and then he kissed her. "I don't think that's a word, miss," he teased.

"It's Mrs. to you," she said, "and it *is* a word."

"Ouch, that hurts." Asa rolled off, holding his chest, feigning pain.

# ❧ 41 ❧

When Asa finished painting, he came down to the kitchen to clean the brush. Nate was sitting on the porch, intermittently dozing and looking at the sports page. "Sox play a double-header tonight," he said.

"I know," Asa replied. "Wish I had tickets."

Nate stood up and took out his wallet. He pulled out several bills and handed them to Asa.

Asa looked at the money. "This is too much."

"Nonsense. You did a great job, and I appreciate it—and I think Noelle enjoyed having you around." He smiled and added, "Besides, all college boys need extra spending money."

"All right. Thanks, Uncle Nate."

Nate reached out to shake Asa's hand. Asa was flustered by a sudden wave of shame and guilt, but he pushed it aside and grasped Nate's hand, realizing how strong and honest his grip felt. "The sill is going to need a second coat. Would you like me to come by tomorrow and finish it?" he asked hopefully.

"There's no need, Asa. I can handle it."

"Okay." Asa hesitated. "Well . . . is Noelle around?" he asked.

"No, she had to run to the store to pick up a few things."

Asa immediately wondered which store. Maybe he could find her—

Nate interrupted his thoughts. "We are definitely planning to come over next week," he said with a grin. "The thirty-first, right?"

Asa nodded. There was no way he could wait that long.

# ❦ 42 ❧

Asa's truck was gone when Noelle returned. With a mixture of relief and disappointment, she carried the groceries up the walk. Hearing her steps, Nate held the screen door and reached for the bags.

"Is there more?"

"No, this is it."

Nate opened the refrigerator and carefully placed each egg into its curved cup. He put away the milk and orange juice, and Noelle gently moved him aside to open the freezer and put away the ice cream.

"Why don't you leave that out and I'll have some with my cobbler?" Noelle took it back out and put it on the counter. Nate lifted off the top. "Do you want some? I'll share," he said with a grin.

"No . . . you have it," she said.

"What's the matter?" he asked.

She forced a smile. "Nothing."

He pulled her into his arms. "It doesn't seem like nothing."

Noelle stiffened as Nate brushed his lips down her neck. He

held her close, and she squeezed her eyes closed and silently pleaded, *Don't cry, don't cry. Whatever you do, don't cry!*

Nate kissed her cheeks and lips. "I've missed you," he whispered.

"I've missed you too," she managed to reply. *Oh, God, what have I done? How am I ever going to do this?*

Nate slowly unbuttoned her blouse, pulled it back, and softly kissed her shoulder. Noelle kept her eyes closed and prayed for forgiveness.

# ❧ 43 ❧

With Martha happily limping beside him, Asa walked along the beach in the late-afternoon sun. Every once in a while, the shiny black head of a seal bobbed above the surf and studied them curiously. Asa watched it until it went under again and then focused on waves farther down the shore, waiting for it to resurface. He smiled and wondered what Noelle was doing at that very moment. *Perhaps making dinner or reading a book on the porch, or maybe she was lying by the pool.* He pictured her, and to his dismay, hoped that she wasn't. *But what if she was? Why should Nate be the one to enjoy looking at her? Why should he be the one to touch her smooth skin? Why is he the one who lies beside her every night? Oh, God, why is he the one who gets to make love to her?*

With shocking clarity, a merciless answer filled Asa's consciousness: *Because he is her husband!* The answer echoed through his mind and blindsided him with yet another wave of jealousy and frustration.

"I don't give a damn!" he shouted back, his fists clenching in fury.

# ❧ 44 ❧

August 31 dawned unexpectedly cool. It had been a chilly night, and the coolness of the morning air whispered of autumn. At breakfast, Samuel teased, "There is an age-old saying, you know. . . ."

Sarah chimed in, "Yes, we know: 'Six weeks from first katy-did to first frost.' Don't remind us! It's still summer!" Then she looked at Asa. "You have another present—why don't you open it?" Asa had already opened several gifts: two wool sweaters, hiking boots, a wool jacket, and a collection of poems by Robert Frost. A second book, a novel, was from his father. *To Kill a Mockingbird* had just come out that summer, and Samuel said he hoped Asa didn't mind that he had read it first.

Asa opened the book and saw his father's inscription. "I've heard about it, Dad. Did you like it?"

"It was very good," Samuel answered thoughtfully. "A good lesson . . ."

Asa looked at all the gifts and then at his mother. "You know, Mom, for someone who says 'It's still summer,' you've certainly created a conflicting theme with these presents!"

"That's true, dear. Look at the things you've given him," Samuel said.

"Well, it gets cold in New Hampshire, and I just want him to be prepared."

"I'm already packed," Asa teased. "I don't have room for these things."

"You'll just have to make room. Now open."

Asa started to open the package from his brother. Martha, who was nosing around the breakfast table, came over to help tear the paper away.

Asa looked at the gift and smiled. *"Sermons and Soda-Water."* He held up the boxed set of three slim volumes for his parents to see.

"John O'Hara," Sarah said thoughtfully.

"It's in case you forget to go to church," Isaac teased.

They all laughed and Sarah eyed him. "You'd better not!"

It felt good to laugh. It had been a long and lonely week. Even though he had spent it surrounded by friends and hanging out at the beach, Asa ached to see Noelle, to be alone with her once more. The week had dragged by, and it tortured him to realize that time was running out. He couldn't think of any excuse to stop by the house, and every time he let himself think of Nate and Noelle alone, it drove him crazy. He tried to write, but nothing would come. Sitting at his desk, he just felt empty and lost and sad. The revolving rhythm of the lighthouse only served to further emphasize the fleeting passage of time.

Samuel stood to clear the plates. "Are you two going to be around today?"

The boys looked at their father, and Isaac replied, "Of course, Dad. Who else will pull the clam bellies for you?" He headed up the stairs to shower.

Sarah turned to Asa. "Are you really all packed?"

Asa leaned back in his chair and felt a wave of anxiety. "I think so," he answered.

"Well, be sure," Samuel said. "We'd like to head out first thing in the morning. Orientation is at two o'clock."

"I still don't see why freshmen have to arrive so much sooner than everyone else," Asa grumbled. "Just think, Dad, if I stayed here and found a job, you wouldn't have two tuitions to think about."

Sarah studied him. She still hadn't been able to put her finger on what was troubling her son, but she couldn't help but think it was the prospect of going away. "Asa, everything will be fine. You'll become adjusted in no time." She followed Samuel into the kitchen, and Asa could hear them quietly talking. He leaned forward to listen.

"I don't know what's gotten into him lately," he heard his mother say. "He's been so moody and withdrawn. I honestly think he's hiding something."

"You worry too much," his father answered. "I'm sure he's just anxious about school. You know he's not like Isaac. He's much quieter . . . and less outgoing. He'll find his way once he gets settled and caught up in a routine." Samuel paused and shook his head. "And I don't know what he could possibly be hiding—I think that's your imagination."

"I hope so," she sighed.

Asa leaned back, closed his eyes, and continued to stroke the noble black head that rested contentedly on his thigh.

## ❧ 45 ❧

Isaac was in the driveway when Jen pulled up in the Corvair. He tucked two beers under a beach blanket and convinced her they should go for a ride before everyone else arrived. Asa seized the opportunity to move his truck down to the parking lot at Nauset Light. He had plans of his own. If anyone asked, he would just say that he was making room for all the cars. He grabbed a bottle of champagne from his father's cellar supply and put it on ice. Placing the cooler on the passenger floor with a blanket thrown over it, he drove the truck down to the parking lot and walked back along the path that passed by the lighthouse.

Samuel was on the porch squeezing a lime into his drink when Asa came up the porch stairs. "Well, what can I get for the birthday boy?" he asked, smiling.

"I'll have what you're having," Asa said, feeling bold and excited by what the evening might hold. Samuel made another drink, held it out to him, and lifted his own glass.

"Happy birthday, Asa," he said, looking his son in the eye.

"May the year ahead be full of blessings, adventure, and high marks!"

Asa laughed. "Thanks, Dad, but you're supposed to say, ' 'Tis the chowdah that warms a man's belly . . .' "

Samuel agreed with a chuckle. "Yes, that too."

They both turned as Martha barked and struggled to pull herself up off the weathered wooden floor.

"Don't you know me yet, you silly old girl?" Nate came up the steps and kissed Martha on the nose. He smiled, shook hands with Sam, and clapped Asa on the shoulder. "Happy birthday, Asa! It's all downhill from here!" He turned to Samuel. "And you—you must be feeling really old!"

Samuel laughed and pointed to his glass. Nate nodded.

"Where's that lovely wife of yours?" Samuel asked, putting ice in a glass for Nate.

"Oh, she's coming. She has her own birthday gift, and she had to 'fix' it," he said, winking at Asa. "Which reminds me." He reached into his pocket for an envelope. "Asa, let me give these to you now before it gets crazy." He held the envelope out to him. "I want you to know, I thought of this all on my own, *and* I had to get special permission from the boss to get you out of school." He winked at Sam. "I hope you won't miss anything too important."

Asa looked puzzled as he opened the envelope and pulled out four tickets. The two men watched as a smile spread across Asa's face.

"Hey! Tickets to the Sox-Orioles game!" He looked at the date. Wednesday afternoon, September 28. "Thanks, Uncle Nate. I'll be there."

"The other tickets are for Isaac, your dad, and me. Isaac will have to miss school and get himself to Fenway too."

"I'm sure that won't be a problem," Sam said.

"You will have to come the farthest," Nate said to Asa. "Hope you won't mind a long bus ride."

"I won't mind. I think that's Ted Williams's last home game. I would travel any distance to be there!"

"You're right." He smiled. "That's why we're going!"

Noelle had gone into the house through the front door to fix Asa's present and now she and Sarah came out onto the porch. Sarah hugged Nate, who was still smiling. "I told you he would like 'em," he said to her.

"Oh, I had no doubt he would *like* them! Just as long as he gets all of his work done," she said, eyeing Asa.

"I will, Mom. Don't worry!"

Noelle stood next to Nate with her hands behind her back. Nate put his arm around her shoulder. "I don't know if your gift is going to be able to beat mine," he teased.

"I don't know either," she teased back with a grin. "We'll just have to see."

Noelle held out an elegantly wrapped package. "Happy birthday, Asa," she said with a twinkle in her dark eyes.

Asa struggled to hide his emotions. "Thanks," he said, fumbling with the ribbon. He finally managed to untie it, and Martha made her way over to help with the wrapping paper. Under the delicate tissue paper was a white cotton T-shirt with forest green piping around the neck and each sleeve. On the left chest, also in green, was the Dartmouth insignia. Asa smiled, lifted the shirt out, and realized that there was something tucked inside. He unfolded the shirt and revealed the worn cover of an old book that he had seen once before. He looked at Noelle in amazement as he reverently picked up the signed copy of *Leaves of Grass* that Noelle's grandfather had given her.

"You shouldn't give this away," he said in disbelief.

"I want you to have it," she said. "That way, I'll always know it's in good hands." She smiled warmly at him, hoping he understood *exactly* what she meant. Asa's parents and Nate seemed oblivious to the deeper meaning of their exchange.

Asa searched Noelle's eyes. He wanted to hold her, to say so much more. Instead, he just smiled and said, "Thank you very much."

"You are very welcome."

Nate broke the silence. "Well, I guess it's a toss-up."

Asa grinned. "You are both very generous. I can't thank you enough."

"Why don't you try on the shirt?" Sarah suggested as Sam handed each of the ladies a glass of wine.

Asa nodded and took the gifts up to his room. He tucked the tickets inside the book and set it on his desk. Then he unbuttoned and pulled off his shirt, threw it on the bed, and pulled on the new one. He glanced in the mirror; it was a good fit.

When he came back down, Isaac and Jen had returned and Nate was telling Isaac about the tickets. "That sounds great. I'm sure I can get away." Isaac elbowed him. "Hey, nice shirt!"

Asa elbowed him back. "Hey, thanks!" He found his drink, took a sip, and looked around for Noelle. She was standing by the stairs. Asa walked over, leaned on the railing, and looked out at the ocean swells. Noelle turned to lean on the railing, too, and her arm brushed against his.

"Be careful," he warned softly, "I can't handle too much bare skin. . . ."

"Mmmm, I know."

"Do you also know"—he hesitated and glanced around—"that I can't get you off my mind?"

"I have that effect on men," she teased.

"I want you so much," he whispered.

Noelle eyed his drink. "I thought you didn't touch that stuff."

Asa looked down at his glass and absently wiped away the drops of condensation.

"I'm throwing caution to the wind."

"Well, you have a long car ride tomorrow. You should take it easy."

He gazed at her. "Noelle, I need to see you alone. Is there any way you can meet me later?"

She heard the longing in his voice and turned to look at him. She couldn't help noticing how tan his face looked against the snowy white of the T-shirt and how bleached the summer sun had made his hair. She realized that he must have just had it cut, because there was a line of fair skin around his neck and in front of his ears.

"Nice haircut," she teased, all the while thinking how good he looked. His eyes searched hers for an answer, and she knew she would have to give him one. She looked away, knowing he would be crushed if she declined.

"Asa, I—"she began to answer, but was interrupted.

"Noelle, Asa, turn around." They turned and a light flashed. Grinning, Isaac said, "Mom wants some pictures—you know, for posterity."

Noelle said, "Well, you can do better than that." She put her arm around Asa, and he draped his arm over her shoulders. They smiled this time, and Isaac snapped the shutter again.

"Okay, perfect. Asa, come on," Isaac called. "The guys are here, and we're going out back." Earlier that afternoon, Isaac and Asa had set up the volleyball net out by the picnic table in the yard. Isaac had also filled a cooler and set up some chairs.

"You'd better go." Noelle nodded after Isaac.

"I will," he said, waiting.

"Asa, I don't know if I can get away, and honestly, I don't know if it's a good idea." She paused and looked around. Then she looked in his eyes. "You have no idea how much I'm going to miss you—*all* of you," she whispered with a sad smile. "And how much I would love to be *with* you again, especially tonight, but then what?" She shook her head and softly murmured, " 'More dark and dark our woes . . .' "

Asa closed his eyes and tried to control his endless roller-coaster ride of emotions.

Noelle put her hand on his shoulder, but then she withdrew it. "It's so hard to stand here and not touch you," she whispered. "Asa, please understand, if I don't come, it's not because I don't love you—it's because I *do*."

He looked into her eyes. "Okay," he said. He finished his drink and turned to go down the stairs.

# ❧ 46 ❧

After the sun went down, an autumn chill swept in. Gradually, the adults pulled on sweaters and migrated inside to warm themselves with another bowl of chowder. The sudden change in temperature surprised everyone and made them realize that the hazy summer days would soon be just a memory. In the cool night air, even the incessant scratching of crickets and katydids slowed. Isaac and Asa had built a fire in the outdoor fireplace, and the kids were all warming their hands and talking about their school plans when Sarah called them in for cake.

Isaac helped light the candles, and Sarah carried the cake in as everyone gathered around to sing. Noelle watched Asa's face in the warm glow of the candles. She looked around at the group of friends who circled him, and her heart ached as she watched Nate across the way, smiling and singing too.

When the song ended, Isaac teased, "Wish for something good!"

Asa hesitated, looked up, and caught Noelle's eye. He gave her a quick half-smile and blew out the candles. In the darkness, Noelle knew what he had wished for, and with all her heart, she wished it could come true.

Cake was being handed around the room when there was a tentative knock at the front door. Samuel opened it and found two pretty young women standing there.

"Hi, I'm Kate. Is Isaac here?"

Samuel invited them in. "He sure is," he said, reaching out his hand. "I'm his dad."

The taller of the two girls took his hand and then introduced her friend. "This is Jess. Isaac told us you were having a party tonight . . . if we wanted to come."

"We are. Come right in and I'll find him."

The girls came in, and Sarah greeted them with a piece of cake. Asa looked over and immediately knew who the taller girl was. She was slender and very pretty. She had long dark hair and was wearing a Boston College sweater. Isaac had described her to a tee. Asa chuckled to himself and wondered just how his brother would handle this one.

Isaac came in, caught Asa's eye, and rubbed his forehead in dismay.

"Hi, Kate. I never expected you to make the trip all the way out here."

Kate smiled. "Well, you've talked so much about it, we just thought it would be fun." She hesitated. "Do you remember Jess?" she asked, motioning to her friend.

"Of course." He turned to Jess and smiled. "I'm glad you could come. I see my mom has already given you some cake. Would you like something to drink?" He motioned to Asa to come over. Isaac introduced them to his brother and then retreated to the kitchen for drinks. Asa tried to strike up a conversation, although he wanted no part of his brother's charade. He didn't want to see Jen's feelings hurt, and at the moment, it seemed inevitable. When Isaac finally returned with drinks, Asa excused himself and ducked out to the porch. With the adults inside and most of the kids back down by the fire, it was deserted.

Asa looked up at the deep blue canvas, splashed with thousands of glittering sparkles, and remembered the countless hours he and Isaac had spent peering into their father's telescope and learning the stars' stories. Asa knew them all. He looked up and found his birthday constellation, recalling the first time Samuel had pointed it out. He could almost hear his father's voice. *"The Archer is your constellation, Asa. The best time to view it is always on your birthday."* His father put his hand on his shoulder and pointed. *"Do you see the stars that look like the Big Dipper, only upside down?"* He pictured himself as a nodding six-year-old. *"That is called the Milk Dipper, and the other name for the Archer is Sagittarius. Do you see the three stars in a curved line that look like a bow?"*

He had nodded again and then shouted excitedly, *"And, Dad, the star to the right makes the arrow!"* Samuel laughed, and while they watched, a small bright star had suddenly raced across the sky. *"Look, Dad, a shooting star!"* Asa had shouted.

Samuel had nodded. *"God must have sent that for you, Asa!"*

Asa smiled at the memory, and it suddenly occurred to him to pray—instead of wish—for what he wanted. But how could he? He had deliberately turned his back on God. He had knowingly, willingly, forsaken everything his parents had taught him, and he hadn't cared about the outcome. Nate had given him an amazing birthday present, and in a heartbeat, he would still betray him again. *What kind of person have I become?*

The screen door opened quietly, and Noelle came out, pulling a sweater around her shoulders.

"I thought I might find you out here. Aren't you cold?"

"No, but I'll keep *you* warm."

She smiled. "We're heading home soon, and I wanted to be sure to get your address at school." She had a piece of paper and pencil ready.

Asa suddenly hated the word *we*. "I don't know it offhand," he said, "but I can get it. Are you leaving right now?"

"Pretty soon."

Asa didn't say anything but looked back at the stars. He wished time would just stop right now. He couldn't bear the thought of tomorrow—and all of the endless, empty days to follow.

"I'll wait for you later on the beach. Do you remember the path?" Asa looked around, reached for Noelle's hand, and drew her into a dark corner of the porch.

"Don't wait—" she began, but he pulled her close and kissed her.

Asa ached for so much more, and in that moment, Noelle would have loved to let him, but the shadows couldn't be trusted. Instead, they offered only torment and sadness.

Suddenly, a sound came from the kitchen, and Noelle quickly pulled away, her heart pounding with fear. Asa leaned back against the wall, closed his eyes, and clenched his fists in frustration and despair.

"Please don't go," Isaac pleaded as Jen came out onto the porch.

"Isaac, I'm really tired." She paused. "Maybe we can talk tomorrow." She turned and headed down the stairs.

Isaac watched her walk away and shook his head. He saw Asa and Noelle standing there. "Asa, if you're smart, you'll just stay away from *all* women," he said, letting the screen door slam. The irony was not lost on his brother.

Noelle stepped back into the shadow and gently wiped a tear from Asa's cheek. He reached up, took her hands in his, and pulled them down to his sides.

"Be careful," he said sadly. "That's what got you in trouble last time."

"I know," she said with a smile. She paused. "Asa . . . please remember everything I said—I meant every word."

Asa returned her sad smile and let go of her hands. "I'll get the address."

"There you are," Nate said. He was standing in the kitchen, talking to Sarah when they came in.

"I was just asking Asa for his address. It's always nice to get mail when you're away from home."

Asa riffled through some papers on the counter and jotted down the address. He handed the piece of paper to Noelle and managed to smile.

"Thank you again for everything." He shook Nate's hand. "I'm looking forward to the game." He turned to Noelle. "Thank *you* for the shirt and the book. The shirt is perfect, and I will always treasure the book."

She gave him a hug, and he closed his eyes. He breathed in deeply and felt the familiar curve of her body. Noelle forced herself to pull away before it seemed too long.

"Good luck at school," she said.

He searched her eyes one last time. *Please don't let this be the last time.*

# 47

"Surely you noticed," Nate said in the darkness of the car.

"Noticed what?" she asked.

"The look in his eyes."

Noelle's heart beat faster. "I don't think so."

"You don't see the way he looks at you?" Nate sounded incredulous.

Noelle thought quickly. *Maybe denial isn't the best strategy.* She laughed lightly. "Well, *you* obviously do, but I'm sure it's only an innocent crush. He'll get over it as soon as he sees his first pretty college girl." She paused and put her hand on his. "Besides, you have nothing to worry about—there's only you."

# 48

Martha picked up her head sleepily when Asa slipped down the stairs. He knelt beside her and scratched her behind the ears.

"I'll be back in a bit," he said softly. She laid her head down and stretched her neck to watch him push open the door. It creaked forbiddingly as he squeezed through. A biting wind blew in off the ocean and whipped at the tablecloth that had been left out, folding it over and threatening to sweep it to the floor. Asa hurried through the darkness to his truck. His heart pounded as he pulled out of the parking lot and switched on the headlights. His mind was racing. *Was Noelle already there? Had she been waiting long? Had she given up and gone home? Was she coming at all? I must get there. Oh, God, please let me see her . . . just once more.*

Route 6 was deserted, and the road leading to Nauset Beach was dark and lonely. Asa parked his truck in the empty lot, grabbed the cooler and blanket, and jogged down the beach until he reached the place where the path came through the tangle of scrub brush. Noelle was not waiting, and Asa prayed that he hadn't missed her. He stood still in the eerie darkness and wondered what he should do. The wind whipped at his thin shirt, and he wished he had thought to bring a jacket. Remembering the matches he still had in his pocket, he looked around for some driftwood.

## ❧ 49 ❧

Clouds rushed across the sky, billowing like curtains in front of the moon. On the desolate beach, a boy gathered enough wood for a small fire. He flipped open a matchbook and saw that three matches remained. He cupped the first two flames in his hands, only to have the laughing wind reach around and steal them away. He looked at the last match and turned his back to the wind, waiting for a gust to pass, and then struck again. Carefully, he held the tiny flicker to the dry grass and watched it slowly catch and start to burn. He dared a tentative smile, but the relentless wind had no mercy for the figure with the flame. It swept around his back to steal again, and the boy just stared at the dark, cold wood. Undaunted, he pulled a blanket around his shoulders and waited.

In the bedroom overlooking the ocean, a woman stood by the window and watched the clouds racing with the wind. The moonlight illuminated the room behind her, and she turned to look at the man as he slept. She thought of the first time she lay beside him. He had made love to her with tears in his eyes, and his tears had made her love him all the more. He was a sound sleeper, she knew. One hot summer night when they were first married, she had tried to wake him with a piece of ice. She had run it along the curve of his spine, and the water had trickled down to the small of his back and made a puddle. She couldn't believe he slept through it, and in the morning, she showed him the damp sheet. He laughed and told her that when he was a boy, his father had turned up the *1812 Overture* as loudly as their old Victrola would play to wake him. More often than not, the neighbors would wake to the sound of booming cannons before he did. She smiled, picturing him as a boy with tousled hair, sleeping through the thundering climax of the famous overture.

She turned to look out the window again and pictured another boy, shivering in the darkness, his heart full of hope and desire. She knew it was possible to slip away unnoticed. She thought of what it would be like to go to him, the surprised smile on his face when he saw her, the feeling of his arms around her, his gentle kiss, his soft touch. She stared sadly out the window and thought of him waiting alone . . . his heart breaking.

The boy trembled under the blanket. He stood for hours, her words echoing in his mind. *If I don't come, it's not because I don't love you—it's because I do.* And his silent reply. *But if I stay, you might still come.*

At last the stars grew dim in the azure sky, and the boy pushed through the underbrush to look up at the window one last time. The house was dark and quiet. It seemed impenetrable and private. He pictured her lying beside the man. Angry, jealous tears burned his eyes as he realized he was just an uninvited intruder. He had no right to be there, he had no reason to stay.

## ∾ 50 ∾

Asa did not know if his parents heard him pull in. He parked the truck on the far side of the house. No one would be using it while he was away. The sky had grown brighter, and the stars had become faint. Still, he hoped no one was awake yet. He kicked off his sand-filled shoes and pushed open the door. Martha's tail thumped against the hardwood floor. He sat down next to her, and she put her head on his lap. He stroked her velvety ears and whispered, "Wish I could take you with me, ole girl." Martha thumped her tail harder and licked his hand. Asa leaned back and thought about the day ahead. He was thankful that he had already put most of his belongings in his father's car. Only his birthday presents and a few small things were left to pack. He heard his parents stirring and gently lifted Martha's head back onto her bed. Then he quickly slipped up the stairs to shower.

By eight o'clock, they were on their way. Isaac and Martha had seen them off. It was far easier for Asa to say good-bye to his brother than it was to say good-bye to Martha. He kissed her on the head. "You know the routine," he whispered. "I'll be back." He shook Isaac's hand. "Keep me posted on all the drama," he said with a wry smile.

"Yeah," Isaac replied with a grimace. He had not had a good night, and he hoped he could resolve the "drama" before he returned to college the following week.

Asa sat in the backseat and looked out at all that was familiar. Every ice-cream shop, vegetable stand, and seafood shanty was wrapped in some boyhood memory. He watched people shopping for fresh clams or lobster or salad for that evening's dinner and realized that he would be far away by that time. He stared at the passing landscape and longed to stay. His father switched on the radio and tuned in an old country station. The deep haunting voice of Johnny Cash drifted through the car. Asa closed his eyes and listened to the sad lyrics about missing someone and wondered if Noelle missed him as much as he missed her.

# PART II

*My sorrow is beyond healing, my heart is faint within me!*
*. . . is there no balm in Gilead?*

—Jeremiah 8:18, 22

# 51

Autumn whispered through the leaves, leaving a blush of rouge along the treetops. Against this tapestry of change, the September sky had a cobalt hue, bluer than that of any summer day. In spite of himself, Asa fell into the routines of college life. For the most part, he kept to himself. He was not at all surprised one afternoon to overhear his roommate complaining that he was a bore. The boy was trying to make arrangements to move in with two other students whose extracurricular activities were a bit more exciting. Asa didn't care. He could certainly understand his roommate's situation. He had never been one to reveal too much about himself, and now he was even less likely. Now, because of his promise to Noelle, no one could ever know the person he had become. He had unwittingly sentenced himself to a lifetime of solitary confinement. He would never be able to share—with anyone—the events that shaped him, and even if he did try someday, he doubted that mere words would ever be enough.

After his roommate finally succeeded in securing different living quarters, Asa became an even more solitary figure in the landscape of freshmen. He threw himself into his schoolwork and rarely socialized. He briefly considered trying out for the cross-country team, but after enduring one testosterone-induced conversation he had while they worked out, he decided that he preferred to run alone. He ran early, slipping out of the silent dorm and into the cool northern air. In the predawn light, he explored the historic campus and the surrounding old New England neighborhoods. He was usually back to his room and showered before any other doors had creaked open. At meals, Asa also sat alone. He kept an open book in front of his tray and maintained a demeanor that was not inviting to passersby.

To Asa's surprise, the days passed quickly, and even though each day seemed to blend into all the rest, there was one daily occurrence that gave him something to look forward to: the delivery of mail. Taking two granite steps at a time into the school post office, Asa would quickly scan the rows of mail slots with small combination locks on their doors. With a tightening in his chest, he would peer through the tiny glass window to see if there were any envelopes leaning up against the inside wall. Noelle had proven true to her word, and after her first letter, Asa had forgiven her for not meeting him that last night. She wrote often—two or three times a week. Asa would slip her envelope into a book and find a seat on the grass under the reaching boughs of an old oak tree or at a worn secluded table by the window in the library. There, with the sun casting light across the pages, he would slowly read, running his fingers over the pale stationery and thinking of the slender hands that had touched it last, the hands that had touched *him* and given him such pleasure.

Noelle's letters were warm and funny and spoke of life at home and at work. She wrote about the changing weather and the ocean and the stars. She wrote about Nate finding a bottle of champagne by the pool—*where in the world had that come from???* And she always closed with thoughts of him—*she missed him, every part of him.* Her thoughts stirred his fire and kept the embers burning. Asa clung to her words, and they sustained him—more than food or drink or air. He lived for these, elegant lines linked together to give him hope.

Asa could not write back. There was no safe address for him to send letters, so he filled his notebook with his thoughts and kept it in a box with her letters. Night after night, he sat by the open window in his room and listened to the wind in the hills. He heard the haunting call of an owl and then a distant reply of interest. He listened to the endless cry of the whip-poor-will and the sad lonely whistle of a freight train. He wrote as if he were writing to her—about these sounds and about the memories he held close, reliving them over and over, burning them into his mind.

Noelle's letters were not the only ones Asa received. There were almost as many from his mother. She, too, wrote about the changing weather and her daily activities. She had continued to stay at the summerhouse because it was her favorite time of year—*so quiet and peaceful, now that all the vacationers have gone home.* While he was out running early in the morning, it was comforting for Asa to know exactly where Sarah could be found at that very moment. He pictured her sitting on the back porch with a blanket wrapped around her shoulders, a hot cup of coffee in one hand and her worn Bible in the other. The day before he was to head to Boston for the game, Asa received a package from his mother. When he pulled away the paper, he found a tin of chocolate chip cookies, a short note, and some photos:

> *Enjoy! Also enclosed are some pictures*
> *from your birthday! Miss you!*
> *Love, Mom*
> *P.S. Martha approves of the cookies and misses you too!*

Asa quickly flipped through the snapshots and then stopped and stared. He had completely forgotten that Isaac had taken pictures of Noelle standing beside him, but there it was, an intimate moment captured and preserved—a moment he could save, and savor, a part of Noelle that was *his* to keep. He looked at her smile and felt her arm around his waist. He smelled the scent of sandalwood soap and felt the cool ocean breeze billowing in off the water. He looked at the picture and thought of the words she had spoken before *and after* the picture was taken.

# 52

The following morning, Asa was up early. He skipped his run, showered and dressed, and grabbed his old Red Sox cap. He tucked the picture of Noelle into the book from his father and put the book, the tin of cookies, and his poetry notebook into his shoulder bag.

It was a cool, overcast day, and Asa was glad that he had remembered his jacket. After hitching a ride to the bus station, he ran across the street for a cup of coffee. Back inside, he paid for a round-trip ticket, climbed onto the bus, and found a seat toward the back. There weren't many travelers leaving Hanover that morning, but Asa figured they would pick up more along the way. He settled into his seat, looked out the window at the changing colors, and thought about the day ahead. He was excited about the game, and he looked forward to seeing some familiar faces. He realized that it wasn't just Noelle he missed.

Asa arrived at South Station and took the T to Fenway. Although he knew his way around Boston, he felt out of place being away from school on a school day. Asa had given two of the tickets to his father, one to Isaac, and had kept the last for himself. Over the weekend, they had spoken on the phone and confirmed the arrangements to meet at their seats. Asa went in and checked behind the Red Sox dugout to make sure he was the only one to arrive early and went to buy a Coke. Drink in hand, he sat down and watched batting practice. Almost immediately, he spotted the # 9 jersey at the plate and smiled. He didn't care if the Sox were having their worst season in twenty years; he was just happy to be there with all the other Hub fans cheering for the Splendid Splinter one last time.

Isaac came up behind him and climbed over the seats with two beers in his hands. He was grinning and singing dramatically along with Fenway's thundering organ.

He glanced at Asa's soda and asked, "What happened to the I.D. I made for you?"

Asa ignored the question. "You should keep your day job," he teased.

The two brothers sat together in the bleachers, drinking beer, watching the players warm up, and reveling in the wonderful freedom of the afternoon. They finished their first beer, and Isaac had just left to get a second round when their father and Nate arrived.

Asa stood to shake hands and offered to go get more drinks. Both men smiled at the idea. "Sounds good," his father answered. He took off his sports coat, rolled up his sleeves, and handed Asa several bills. The two men sat down, and Asa retreated to the refreshment stand to find Isaac. A short time later, the boys returned with four foot-long hot dogs and four overflowing cups.

Isaac smiled. "It doesn't get any better than this! Thanks, Uncle Nate!"

Asa nodded in agreement, taking a bite of his hot dog.

Samuel and Nate asked the boys how school was going and, after a while, broke off into a conversation of their own. Asa listened halfheartedly until he heard Samuel ask about Noelle.

By this time, the ballpark had filled to near capacity, and it was difficult to hear Nate's answer. Asa strained to listen.

"She's fine. Did I tell you she took a full-time position at the hospital? Starting next week—" Nate was interrupted by cheering fans as the Red Sox came out onto the field. When the noise finally faded, he continued. "She's out at the Cape right now. She was hoping the weather would be better."

Asa's heart raced. He thought of Noelle alone at the Cape house and could barely wrap his mind around the possibilities. Just then, Isaac elbowed him.

"Hey, Asa! Have you heard anything I just said?"

"Yup, I heard you," Asa answered, his heart still pounding. "You said you need to use the john and get a refill—whenever you're ready." He followed his brother up the steps and tried to remember which classes he would miss.

The cloudy skies over Boston seemed to fit the mood of Red Sox fans that bittersweet afternoon. Their hero was retiring but not without one last hurrah. It was a good game, even though the Sox were trailing. Asa watched in awe as Ted Williams came up to the plate again. Then, there it was, a 1-1 pitch and the legend drove it 450 feet into the right centerfield seats. The crowd was on their feet as he rounded the bases after his 521 home run.

Finally, in the ninth inning, Ted Williams headed out to left field for the last time. He was immediately replaced by Carroll Hardy. At that moment, "MisTer Wonderful" retired, and the cheering fans were on their feet again. Asa felt tears stinging his eyes. He looked over at his father, smiling and clapping. He watched Nate cheering beside him, and then Nate caught his eye. With a smile, he winked and gave Asa a thumbs-up. Asa smiled, too, and again thought about how, even after the amazing gift of this day, he was capable of betraying Nate. The Sox rallied in the ninth for two more runs and beat the Orioles 5 to 4.

# 53

Samuel and Nate dropped the boys off at South Station. On the way, Samuel asked Asa if he had had a chance to read the book he had given him. Asa replied that he had finished it on the bus ride down. Then Samuel started to tell Nate about "the first book written by a new young talent." As they pulled up in front of the historic station, Nate slipped each of the boys a folded bill. They thanked him and said they hoped to see him at Thanksgiving. Then they said good-bye to their father and promised to call soon.

Isaac's bus was due to leave Boston earlier than the bus heading to Manchester. But Asa was eyeing the wooden schedule board for a different destination. He found what he was looking for: "Hyannis—5:45P."

The boys found seats in the busy terminal while they waited for their buses. Asa was antsy, hoping that Isaac's bus would be on time. If it wasn't, he wouldn't be able to carry out his plan. Finally, when Isaac got up to use the men's room, Asa bolted to the ticket counter. Uncertain of the outcome, he unfolded the bill Nate had given him and, suppressing any sense of morality, purchased a ticket to Hyannis. When Isaac returned, his bus was boarding. Asa had his hands in his pockets and was standing near the door, looking out at the buses. The parking spot next to the Providence bus was still vacant, and Asa was relieved. He shook hands with his brother and then made a show of sitting back down to wait for the Manchester bus, not scheduled to depart until 6:10.

Soon after Isaac's departure, a second bus pulled into the vacancy. Hanging in the top of the front window was a sign indicating that its destination was Hyannis. Hanging in the window of the bus beside it was a sign for Manchester. Asa looked at the two buses. He had tickets in his pocket for both of them, and he had only a few minutes to decide. *Would she be happy to see me?* He pictured the surprise on her face and felt her arms around him, and he thought about lying beside her again. . . .

## ❧ 54 ❧

An hour later, Asa looked out at the boats on the canal as the bus crossed over the Bourne Bridge. On any summer Saturday, traffic onto the bridge would be backed up for miles, but on a Wednesday evening in September, there were almost no travelers. The sun was setting behind him, and the light gave a rosy cast to the tops of the trees. As the bus reached the Cape side, Asa's heart filled with the comfortable warmth of being home. Less than a month ago, he had crossed this bridge with a heavy heart, but now, here he was, looking out again at the world of his childhood. It had not changed in his absence, it had only been faithfully waiting to welcome him back.

Asa stepped off the bus in Hyannis, slung his bag over his shoulder, zipped up his jacket, and started walking backward along Route 28. He had considered calling Noelle for a ride but had decided that that would take away from the surprise. So he put his thumb out, and before long, he was huddled in the back of a pickup truck with a big happy-go-lucky golden retriever. The driver and his two young sons were on their way home to Wellfleet and were willing to take Asa all the way to Orleans.

When they arrived, Asa hopped down, gave his hand warmer one last scratch under his chin, thanked the driver, and turned to walk down the winding Beach Road.

More than once along the way, Asa second-guessed the decision he had made in the bus station. But now it was getting late—too late to change his mind—and he picked up his pace. The road was dark and lonely, much like the last time when he had driven down it alone. He pushed the painful memory aside and hoped that tonight would be different. As he walked up the sandy driveway, he could see the outline of the familiar old house and chimney. There were no lights on in the front, and Asa's heart pounded in his chest and kept time with a throbbing in his temple. He walked around back and was thankful to see the back porch sparkling in the warm glow of Christmas lights. The window in the kitchen was also bright and welcoming.

# 55

Asa knocked quietly on the screen door—the last thing he wanted to do was frighten her. He waited, feeling foolish, and then knocked again. This time, she heard his knock and opened the kitchen door. She looked out, trying to see into the darkness through the screen.

"Hey," Asa said softly.

Suddenly, Noelle realized who was standing on her back steps. "Oh, my! Asa, is that you?" She unlatched and pushed open the screen door, and he stepped onto the porch. She looked into his eyes, and a warm, genuine smile spread across her face. "I'm *so* glad to see you."

He sank into her arms and closed his eyes in amazed relief.

They didn't talk. She didn't ask him how or why; she just held him. He could hear faint music coming from the record player in the living room. The smooth, sad voice of Nat King Cole drifted out to where they stood. She took his hand, and he followed her. There were embers glowing in the stone fireplace, and he watched as she leaned over to give them a stir and add more wood. The fire licked upward, and the amber light danced on the walls. Asa felt a chill in spite of its warmth.

Noelle ran her fingers lightly along his cheek and slowly unzipped his jacket. Asa didn't move. He just stood there with his arms hanging at his sides. He allowed her to do whatever she wished—he had no will, no control. She knew why he had come. Noelle brushed her lips against his skin and teased him with her tongue as she slowly unbuttoned his shirt and the top button of his jeans. She slipped her hands inside his shirt, and he felt her warm touch and searched her dark eyes. He knew he would follow her anywhere, would do *anything* she asked. He had lost all sense of self. Nothing mattered, nothing at all, *except being here.*

The haunting lyrics drifted along, and Noelle put her cheek against his chest. They swayed back and forth. She leaned back and pressed her body against him. With trembling hands, Asa lifted her sweater over her head. He kissed her neck and breathed deeply, drinking in her lovely scent, as if his thirst would never be satisfied. In the soft light of the fire, he watched her slip her jeans down. Her body was still tan from the summer sun, and her hair fell across her face when she leaned over.

She reached for him, and Asa lay beside her, watching the firelight dance on the ceiling. The heat from the flames finally warmed his bare skin, and Noelle ran her fingers lightly along the outline of his fading tan lines. She slipped her leg across his bare thighs, and Asa reached down and gently pulled her on top of him. As she moved slowly back and forth, he still couldn't believe what was happening. She smiled and teasingly lifted herself slightly above him. Barely able to hold on, Asa slid his hands from her breasts, pulled her hips down, and lifted his head to watch the movement between their bodies.

## ❧ 56 ❧

As the night stretched toward dawn, the fire was repeatedly rekindled and the energy of their bodies renewed. They were driven by insatiable desire and desperate defiance of the world in which they were trapped. Finally, the flames died down, leaving a bed of glowing embers. Asa lay on his side and watched them burn. Noelle had fallen asleep, and he watched her slow, easy breathing. In the warm glow of the flickering light, his eyes lingered over each shadow cast by the soft curves of her body. Suddenly, a spark from an ember shot upward and was drawn into the rising air. Asa watched it disappear, and then his eyes were drawn to two small hooks that had been tapped into the mantel shelf.

A sudden wave of memories washed over him as he remembered those hooks. He glanced into the adjacent room and saw Annie's piano standing silently in the darkness, and he wondered how long had it been since someone had lifted its cover and brought its lovely sound to life.

Asa closed his eyes and listened; he could almost hear merry laughter and the sound of his father's deep baritone voice blending with Nate's tenor as they sang "We Three Kings of Orient Are," and then he heard his mother's and Annie's soprano voices singing "What Child Is This?". Asa smiled at the memory. As a boy, he had been mesmerized by Annie's nimble fingers dancing along the keys. Oh, the beautiful sounds she could make! And then there was her Christmas Eve dinner—Rock Cornish hens, one for each of them; sweet potatoes; apricot stuffing; crisp green beans; and pickles that tasted like summer. And the pies! Pumpkin, apple, and sweet pecan with whipped cream—everyone had a "sliver" of each.

With no children of their own, Nate and Annie had lavished gifts on the two sons of their dearest friends. Isaac and Asa had even hung Christmas stockings that Annie had made for them on the hooks on the mantel. The boys would sit on the braided rug in front of the fireplace and pull gift after gift from the bulging stockings—elegantly wrapped Christmas stars, flashlights, pocket knives, matchbox cars, silver dollars, peppermints, strings of red licorice, and, of course, from the toes of the stockings, sweet juicy oranges.

Asa opened his eyes, and as quickly as they had come, his childhood memories disappeared. It seemed an eternity ago that he had sat in this very spot in front of the fire and opened gifts. As a boy, he had been cloaked in the comforting and unconditional love of family and friends. Now, as a young man, he was naked, vulnerable, and no longer worthy of such forgiving love. His sacred childhood memories were tainted by betrayal, desire, and the image of his body intertwined with another. He stared into the flames and wondered if Annie could see him now. *Would she ever forgive me?* Asa thought of his old friend and for the first time, felt deeply ashamed.

Noelle stirred beside him. She slipped her hand into his, and he felt its warmth. He wanted to never let it go. He looked down and she opened her eyes and stretched.

"Did you sleep?" she asked.

"No, but you did."

"Mmmm," she murmured lazily.

"*And* you let the fire go out."

"It's not out," she said, reaching for him. "See?"

He smiled sheepishly, pushing aside all thoughts of shame, and pulled her close. "You're right about that. . . ."

# 57

As the morning sun peeked over the edge of the ocean, Noelle turned to look at Asa, who had finally fallen asleep. She eased away and gently covered him with the soft afghan that was draped over the back of the sofa. Noelle had never asked Nate about the blanket, but she had always surmised that it was Annie's handiwork.

Slipping on Asa's shirt, she went into the kitchen to make coffee. While it brewed, she pulled his collar up and breathed in. She loved the smell of his body and the aftershave he wore. She sighed and poured herself a cup of coffee. Cradling the hot cup in her hands, she looked out the kitchen window at the bird feeder. In recent weeks, Noelle had become obsessed with replenishing the feeder. It had even occurred to her that the birds would not survive the winter without her care, but Nate had assured her that there were plenty of year-round residents who kept their feeders filled. As she watched, a pair of cardinals fluttered back and forth between the feeder and a nearby oak tree. In the early light, she noticed another bird in the thicket that she didn't recognize. It was light gray with a black and white pattern on its wings. It didn't come to the feeder but just watched the cardinals' activity. Through the window, she listened to its occasional song and noticed that it was never the same. First it whistled clearly, and then it made harsh, guttural sounds. After that, it sang something entirely different. Puzzled, she returned to the living room in search of Nate's bird book. When she did, Asa looked up sleepily and smiled.

"Nice shirt."

"Thanks," she replied with a grin. "Hey, how are you at identifying birds?"

"Not very good. Why?"

"Well, there's one out back that I've never seen before."

Asa stood up and folded the blanket. Noelle glanced up from her search and watched him. He neatly laid the blanket on the end of the sofa and turned to find his boxers. As he did, he noticed that she was watching him. He turned his back to her with a grin. "There's no peeking!" he said, pulling on his shorts.

"Just admiring," she replied. "By the way, did you want to take a shower?"

"Do you mean *with you?*" he asked hopefully.

"Well, I hadn't thought of that, but you never know," she teased. "What time do you have to be back?"

He came up behind her and put his arms around her. "I was thinking of never going back."

"That sounds enticing. . . . However . . ." She didn't finish.

They went into the kitchen, and Asa poured a cup of coffee and looked out into the yard to where Noelle was pointing. "There it is." She flipped through the bird book, looking for a matching picture. She paused at *Gray Catbird,* and Asa peered over her shoulder.

He shook his head. "No, that one's too gray." Noelle turned the page, and Asa looked at the picture and back out the window. "That's it!" he said. "Look at the wings."

Noelle nodded in agreement. "Hmmm, northern mockingbird. I've always wondered what a mockingbird looked like." She started to read out loud: " 'Sings its loud, clear, complicated songs almost year-round, even at night in spring and summer.' "

Asa took a sip of his coffee and seemed lost in thought. "That's funny," he began. "I just read a book called *To Kill a Mockingbird*. In the book, one of the characters says it's a sin to kill a mockingbird, because all they do is sing." Asa looked around for his shoulder bag. "I have it with me. Maybe you'd like to read it." He found his bag, pulled out the book, ran his hand over the simple light brown cover, and handed it to Noelle. "It was very good."

Noelle opened the book and skimmed the front leaf. She paused and looked up at him. "I will read it. Thanks." Putting it down on the counter, she added, "But now, as much as I would love for you to stay, we really have to think about getting you back to school." She hesitated. "I was going home today anyway, so I can give you a ride to the station. Do you know the bus schedule?"

Asa shook his head. "It doesn't matter. I'll just wait."

"Don't look so gloomy," Noelle said, putting her arms around him. "It's not the end of the world. Besides, I'm still waiting for you to go warm up the shower." Asa closed his eyes and knew he would always want this moment back. . . .

# 58

Late Thursday morning, Nate walked across Dewey Square on his way to meet a client for lunch. He glanced at his watch and realized he was early. He looked around and spotted a corner shop with an illuminated neon coffee cup in the window. He went inside. The shop, with its close proximity to the bus station, was filled with travelers, and the warm air inside had the heady aroma of sweet rolls and cinnamon. Nate took off his overcoat and stood in line. He looked out across the square to South Station and remembered yesterday's baseball game. It had been a great afternoon, and he hoped the boys had gotten back to school without any trouble.

Finally, with a cup of hot coffee in hand, he stepped back out to the curb and stopped to take a sip. As he did, he noticed a turquoise and white Bel Air pull up in front of the bus station. He hesitated curiously and strained to see who was driving. After a few minutes, the passenger door opened and Nate decided he was mistaken. *She certainly wouldn't have a passenger. . . .*

Strangely intrigued, though, he continued to watch. Someone was getting out, but just as they did, a bus pulled around the corner and stopped, blocking his view. Nate waited until the bus finally pulled away but, by then, the car was gone. He shook his head and glanced at his watch again. *There must be countless turquoise Bel Airs in Boston.*

# ❦ 59 ❦

Asa looked up at the departure board and realized he had a long wait ahead of him. He went back outside and looked around. With several hours to kill, he wandered over to a newsstand and glanced at the periodicals. A portrait of Massachusetts's own Henry Cabot Lodge Jr. graced the current issue of *Time* magazine. Lodge, Asa knew, was Nixon's running mate and the biggest surprise of the presidential race. Asa studied the painting and wondered how Massachusetts would decide between Lodge and their young Democratic senator, John F. Kennedy.

He turned to go back inside South Station but changed his mind. He and Noelle had stopped at a diner for breakfast before leaving the Cape, but he was hungry again and decided to look for a place to grab a snack. On the north side of Dewey Square, he noticed a tiny bookstore that was tucked in next to a coffee shop. He hesitated but finally headed in that direction. He went into the bookstore first and halfheartedly perused the new fiction section, looking for something to read on the bus. His eyes were immediately drawn to the now-familiar illustration of a simple tree on a light brown background. Beside it on the shelf was another book with a tree on its cover. On this cover, however, the gnarled and leafless tree was more detailed, and in the shadow of the tree stood a somber boy with his hands in his pockets. The cover had a completely different feeling. Asa picked up the book and scanned the summary. It was about two friends at a boarding school in New Hampshire. Intrigued, he paid for it and headed next door for a cup of coffee and a sweet roll. He had no idea if he would be back at school in time for dinner.

# ❧ 60 ❧

Nate returned home in the late afternoon. The comforting aroma of simmering vegetables and beef filled the kitchen. He lifted the cover off the pot on the stove, and a cloud of steam rolled over its brim. He peered inside at a hearty mixture of tomatoes, peas, carrots, potatoes, and tender chunks of meat; his mouth watered. He threw his jacket over the back of a kitchen chair and walked down the hall of the old Victorian house, sifting through the mail. At the bottom of the stairs, he listened. Noelle was in the shower. Nate returned to the kitchen, opened a bottle of wine, and poured two glasses. He went upstairs and knocked softly on the door. Noelle looked around the curtain as he came in, and he smiled and held a glass out to her.

"Thanks," she said, forcing a smile. She let the curtain stay open at the top, stepped back under the warm water, took a sip, and silently pleaded with herself, *Don't think . . . don't think . . .*

"No, thank *you*," Nate teased, peering around the curtain. "Dinner smells good. Is it almost ready?"

"The carrots need a little longer." He stepped back and

Noelle took a long drink and squeezed her eyes shut. *God, how can I do this to us?*

Nate looked out the window at the setting sun. "Are you almost done?"

"Almost." She finished her drink and turned off the water. When she opened the curtain, he took her glass and handed her a towel.

"How was the Cape?"

"Well, the weather could have been better. How was the game?" She and Asa had talked only briefly about the game.

"It was great. Sox won." Nate watched her dry off and stepped toward her. He draped the towel around her back and gently pulled her toward him. She closed her eyes and silently pleaded, *Not yet, please, not so soon . . .*

# 61

The autumn sky was streaked with orange and pink clouds when the bus pulled into Hanover. Asa climbed down, glanced at his watch, and started to walk. It was chilly, and he knew he probably wouldn't make it back to campus in time for dinner. It didn't matter. He wasn't very hungry. He kicked through the leaves and thought about Noelle. He wondered what she was doing, and his heart ached. *Why does it have to be this way?*

## ❧ 62 ❧

As Nate dozed contentedly, Noelle slipped from between the satin sheets and stole softly down the stairs to check on the stew. The sun had gone down, and the kitchen was dark. Through the window, one thin streak of the fiery orange light burned like an angry wound behind the silhouetted landscape. She refilled her glass and, with tears streaming down her cheeks, stared at the last remnant of this unimaginable day. "God help me," she whispered. "Forgive me for everything I've done. . . ."

Finally, she turned on the stove light, and the shred of bright sky outside was swallowed by blackness. She dried her tears, turned off the stew, and put rolls in the oven to warm. She took out the salad she had made earlier, set the table, and lit candles. Then she went to the bottom of the stairs, called up to Nate, and asked him to bring down the sweater that was in her bag.

A few minutes later, Nate appeared holding her sweater in one hand and his empty glass in the other. He had changed into faded jeans and a soft flannel shirt. She noticed that his hair was getting longer, and it was becoming more salt than pepper.

"Thanks," she said, putting it on. He studied her eyes and gave her a sad smile but didn't reply. Instead, he turned to refill his glass and stared out the window into the darkness. Noelle put on the sweater and still felt chilled. She looked at his back, hoping for some sign of reassurance, but he offered none. "Are you hungry?" she asked, taking the top off the pot and picking up the ladle. He shrugged and took a sip. Her heart was pounding as she filled the two bowls. "What's the matter?" she asked, setting them on the table.

"Nothing," he replied.

Noelle sat across from him, her mind racing with the possibilities. She tried to remain calm, but her stomach was churning so much that she could barely eat. Silently, she tried to reassure herself that it was just her guilt-ridden conscience magnifying his subdued mood. She attempted to lift his spirits with small talk, and he finally became a little more animated. He told her the stew was delicious and even offered to do the dishes. Noelle was relieved; she began to believe that maybe it really was "nothing."

After dinner, Nate was true to his word. He started to clear the table, and Noelle stood to help. She wrapped up the leftovers, put them away, and then went upstairs to finish unpacking.

She turned on the bedroom light and looked at the bedsheets strewn about. She had not knelt beside her bed since she was a little girl. But tonight, more than ever before, she was thankful. She quietly knelt down and bowed her head. Silently, she promised to never let it happen again. Silently, she implored God to always protect Nate from the truth.

After several minutes, she got up to unpack. Her bag was open, and she immediately saw the book Asa had given her resting on top of her belongings. She had forgotten all about it. Now her heart raced as she lifted it out. She opened it, and for the first time, noticed the inscription Samuel had written. She also found the photograph that had been tucked inside the cover. Through a blur of tears, she stared at the image. Her hands were shaking as she closed the book. The thankful relief she had felt just a moment ago was suddenly shattered by fear.

# ⤜ 63 ⤛

Every night before he went to bed, Asa crossed off the date on the calendar above his desk. Every day, as he walked to class, he listened to the autumn wind whisper of winter.

Noelle continued to write, but Asa sensed that something was different. Instead of giving him hope, her letters left him feeling uneasy. He began to notice that she rarely alluded to missing him in a sensual way. In the beginning, she had teased him with her words, and he had hung on to their meaning. Now the absence of these words made him anxious. *Had her feelings changed? Had something happened? Did Nate know?*

Asa punished himself with worry. He found it hard to focus on schoolwork and his appetite waned. He skipped meals and ran instead—running was the only way to escape his self-inflicted misery. As the weeks passed, he found himself tightening his belt an extra notch or two and by mid-November, when he stepped onto a scale in the boys' shower room, he was surprised to discover that he had lost ten pounds.

## ⤚ 64 ⤙

By mid-November, Noelle had settled into her new job at Boston General. She liked it well enough, but by the end of the day, she was exhausted. Nate tried to convince her to work only part-time hours, but she told him that she liked to keep busy. As always, he helped around the house and even made dinner once or twice a week. If he had seen Asa's book in her bag, he never mentioned it. Noelle had immediately tucked it away and read it only when she was home alone. She made every effort to please Nate, and the fleeting, dark mood that had caused her so much alarm was never repeated. She was determined to protect him and resolved to find time at Thanksgiving to gently end the intimacy in her relationship with Asa. She prayed that it would not destroy their friendship, and she prayed that he would be okay. . . .

## ❧ 65 ❧

As Thanksgiving approached, Asa's mood was buoyed by hope and anticipation. He had no idea if there would be an opportunity to be alone with Noelle, but at the very least, he would see her.

On the Wednesday before the holiday, Isaac and Asa arrived home within an hour of each other. Sarah was busy making pies when they came in. They each carried a duffel bag full of laundry, but she didn't care—she was just happy to have her boys at home. Martha was happy too. When Asa pushed open the door, she struggled to pull herself off the slippery linoleum, and her tail wagged so hard that her whole hind end wiggled. Asa set down his things and hugged her first, even before hugging his flour-covered mother. The warm kitchen smelled of apples and cinnamon, cloves and pumpkin, and the windows were steamed over.

Asa washed up and sat down at the kitchen table. Martha rested her head in his lap and closed her eyes with a contented sigh. Sarah set a generous slice of warm apple pie and a large glass of milk in front of her younger son.

"I thought this was for tomorrow," he said in surprise.

"I'm making another," she replied, kissing the top of his head. "Besides"—she looked him over—"you look as if you can use it!"

While he ate, they chatted about school and the weather.

Finally, the conversation turned to Thanksgiving. Asa slipped Martha a piece of piecrust and ventured nonchalantly, "Is Uncle Nate coming?"

"I'm not sure," Sarah answered as she deftly draped smooth piecrust dough over her rolling pin and eased it onto a waiting pie plate. "Noelle hasn't been feeling well." She paused as she pressed the crust into place and began to pinch the edge into a decorative pattern. "Nate's going to call in the morning."

Asa's heart sank. *What if she doesn't come?*

## 66

That evening, Asa had planned to relax at home, but Isaac had other ideas and convinced Asa to go to Haymarket with him and reminded him to bring his I.D. The two brothers stopped for drinks at an old favorite haunt before they ended up at a new pub that seemed to be more popular with the college crowd home for the holiday. It was a packed house, but they managed to get a table in the bar, and pretty soon, a pretty waitress came over to take their order. Isaac flirted with her before finally ordering his usual gin and tonic. Asa started to order another beer, but feeling a bit reckless after the first two, changed his mind and said he'd have the same. The waitress smiled at him warmly, and as she walked away, Isaac teased him, "Man, I think she likes you!"

Asa laughed. "Yeah, right."

"Well," Isaac began, "on that subject, have you found a woman up there in the woods yet?" He hesitated. "Oh, that's right, I forgot—you're still at an all-boys school. Didn't you get enough of that at the Gunnery?"

Asa ignored the remark and absently wiped the outside of

his glass. "Whatd'ya mean 'yet'?" he finally answered with a smile.

Isaac raised his eyebrows questioningly. "What . . . are you holding out on me?"

"Nah, I'd never do that."

"Well?"

"Well yourself," Asa said, changing the subject. "What's new in your *overactive* love life? Are you still with Kate? Or is it Jen?"

Isaac laughed knowingly. "*That* was out of hand!" He paused and took a sip of his drink. "Actually . . . there's someone new."

"That's a surprise," Asa said with a grin.

"I met her at school. She's an illustration major, and"—he grinned—"she's a redhead!"

Asa laughed and teased him, "Yes, but is she a *real* redhead?"

Isaac nodded and winked. "Yup, a real redhead!"

Asa felt light-headed as he lifted his glass. "Well, here's to redheads!"

Isaac laughed, too, clinked his brother's glass, finished his drink, and looked around for the waitress. Catching her eye, he held up his empty glass, pointed at it, and raised two fingers. The waitress nodded.

Asa woke up with a pounding head the next morning. *Never again,* he swore, and went in search of some aspirin. He could hear his mother on the phone as he rummaged through the medicine cabinet. He paused to listen. "It's okay," she said. "Please tell her we hope she feels better." Asa leaned on the sink and looked at himself in the mirror. *She isn't coming.* He stared at his reflection and wondered how he would manage. *Doesn't she know how much I need to see her? Doesn't she want to see me? Maybe she's just making this up. Maybe she doesn't want to see me—or maybe Nate knows and has forbidden her.* Asa punished himself with renewed worry. *God, if I could only see her, just to know that everything is okay.* He fumbled with the bottle, dumped four aspirin into his hand, swallowed them with a splash of water, cursed his brother, fell back into bed, and buried his head under his pillow.

## 67

On Monday night after he had returned to school, Asa was in his room trying to study when he heard the pay phone down the hall ringing. He heard a door open and someone hurrying to answer it. Then he heard a muffled greeting and footfalls coming back down the hall, stopping outside his door. There was a hesitant knock and a voice. "Phone."

"Okay, thanks," he called. Asa's heart pounded as he walked down the hall. He rarely received phone calls. In fact, he was surprised that the student who had answered it even knew which room he was in. He wondered hopefully if the caller was Noelle.

He picked up the receiver.

"Asa?" It was his father. Asa was disappointed, but his heart still pounded. *Why is Dad calling?*

"Hi, Dad."

"Hello, son." His father's voice sounded oddly strained.

"Dad, what's the matter?" Asa's mind began to race.

Samuel hesitated. "Asa, I'm afraid I have some bad news."

Asa tried to swallow the lump in his throat. "I wish I could be there to tell you this . . . and I hope you'll be okay."

"What is it, Dad?" Asa's hands began to shake as he pressed the phone against his ear.

"Asa"—he paused—"Martha has died." Tears welled up in Asa's eyes as he listened. "This morning your mother called her and she didn't come. So she went to look for her. She looked all around the downstairs because it's been so long since Martha had been upstairs. But she couldn't find her, so she finally went up, and there she found her, curled up on the rug next to your bed." His father paused, listening. "Asa . . . are you there?" Tears were streaming down Asa's cheeks. He tried to answer but only a sob came out. "Son, I'm so sorry. Your mother wanted to drive up there to tell you. She is very upset, as we both are. Martha was such a good dog, and she loved you more than anyone."

Asa could not believe his ears. How could this be? Just yesterday, he had held her noble black head in his hands and scratched her white muzzle. He pictured her sweet brown eyes, cloudy with age, gazing after him through the window, and he sobbed again.

"Asa, are you okay?"

"Yes," he choked out.

"We've been thinking all day about what would be best, and your mother thinks we should bury her out at the Cape—near the garden. Would that be all right with you?"

Asa nodded and tried to answer.

"I made a wooden box," he continued, "and we are thinking of going out tomorrow. I know you would want to be there, but you were just home, and we think it's too far. . . ." Asa nodded again. "Hang on," his father continued, "your mother wants to talk to you. Here she is."

"Oh, Asa," she began. Asa could tell she was crying. "I'm so sorry, honey. Are you okay?"

Asa nodded and tried to answer. His mother reiterated her thoughts, and Asa agreed, but then he couldn't listen anymore, he just wanted to hang up the phone. Finally, he convinced his mother that he would be okay and slowly put the receiver back in its cradle. He pulled himself together and walked back down the hall to his room. Then he quietly closed the door behind him, leaned against it, and slid to the floor. Burying his face in his hands, he wondered if dogs knew when the end was near. He wondered if Martha had known yesterday when she watched him leave that it was the last time. Again, he pictured her gazing out the window after him, and a new flood of tears streamed down his cheeks. Maybe God was punishing him, he thought. He certainly deserved it. In despair and frustration, he ran his fists through his hair and wondered how much more he could bear.

# 68

Asa skipped classes the next day. He pulled on the wool jacket his parents had given him and wandered out toward the athletic fields. Dark gray clouds blanketed the sky, and a biting wind scattered about the spits of snow falling. Asa pictured his parents and the task they faced that day, and hot tears welled up again in his red-rimmed eyes. *I should've gone home. It isn't too far,* he thought. As he walked along, he stumbled upon a footpath that he hadn't noticed before. The path left the athletic fields and wandered along the main road for a stretch before it turned into the woods at a trail marker. Asa studied the marker and realized that the path was part of the Appalachian Trail. He had often heard about the famous trail, but he'd never realized that it wandered through Hanover. He had also heard of people who had hiked the entire length of the trail, and then he recalled the haggard-looking backpackers he'd seen in town several months earlier. Today, however, it was just a deserted, lonely path in the woods.

Asa hesitated. He had no idea where the trail led. He wasn't dressed properly; he wasn't prepared for any mishaps in the woods. If anything happened, no one would know where he was. Still, he was drawn into the unfamiliar woods—into the uncertainty and into escaping the punishing world that had become his life. Asa pulled his collar up, thrust his hands in his pockets, and left the road behind.

At the outset, the terrain was easy and the trail headed west. Asa kept his eye on the markers and made good time. Initially, he hiked along frozen wetlands, but by midafternoon, he passed a sign for Goodwin Forest and the terrain became more difficult. As he hiked, large, wet flakes began to fall, then turned into a heavier mix. It occurred to Asa that he should turn around, but he shunned the thought; he wasn't ready—he hadn't learned anything. He was still mired in selfish misery. He grieved the loss of Martha, but even more, he grieved for what he could not have.

Somewhere deep inside, a voice screamed to be heard, trying to tell him that he had it all wrong on this sorrowful day, telling him to set aside his stupid selfishness and give undivided honor to the memory of his beloved dog. Asa trudged along, bent against the bitter, whipping wind, and thought about Martha's unquestioning faithfulness.

He suddenly stopped and looked around. The tree limbs and the frozen ground were covered with snow and were now indistinct. *I'm going to get lost,* he thought, and then it occurred to him, *Maybe it would be better this way. No more pain and jealousy. No more betrayal and deception. No more loneliness and sorrow.* The telling words from Frost's well-known poem ran through his mind: *"These woods are lovely, dark, and deep."* Asa shivered, bowed his head, and pressed on through the squall until finally, just as it began to get dark, he came to a road.

## 69

The weeks between Thanksgiving and Christmas were a blur of studying and exams. Asa's grades had plummeted with his mood, and he knew he needed to do well on his finals. His parents would expect no less. He tried to focus and continually reminded himself that it would be only a few weeks before he saw Noelle again. . . .

He looked forward to being home. At the same time, though, he dreaded that first time he would push open the door and find no wagging tail to greet him, no sloppy kisses to welcome him. The day finally came, and just as he expected, the house full of people seemed strangely empty. At every turn, Asa expected to see his old pal curled up cozily near the wood stove or nosing around the dinner table looking for treats. Instead, he felt her loss with renewed keenness.

On the morning of Christmas Eve, Asa and Isaac helped load the back of the Nomad with pies, Christmas cookies, suitcases, and all the essentials for several days on the Cape. The trunk was almost full when Sarah pointed to a mountain of elegantly wrapped gifts stacked on the dining room table.

"Mom," Isaac protested, "those are *not* going to fit."

"Yes, they are," she replied. "And if they don't, we'll just have to put them on your seat and you can stay home," she replied.

Asa held one box up to his ear, looked at the label, and, with a grin, gave it a shake.

"None of that!" she scolded.

The boys sighed and carried part of the pile out to the car. Asa started to take everything out of the trunk for rearranging as Isaac headed back inside for more boxes. It took the better part of an hour, but they finally managed to fit all of the gifts in the trunk.

## 70

Heat rushed out of the oven when Noelle opened the door to baste the turkey again. The whole house was filled with the comforting aroma of sweet potatoes, melting brown sugar, and of course, turkey. She shut the door and looked in the living room. The Christmas tree glittered brightly in the corner, and Nate's back was turned away as he knelt down in front of the fireplace. She watched him place each piece of wood carefully in the fireplace and began to grow anxious. She was worried about seeing Asa again—and worried about having both Nate and Asa in the same room. She needed to find time to talk to Asa alone; she had so many things to tell him. She looked out the window and silently prayed for the opportunity.

Nate came into the kitchen, dipped a fat shrimp into the cocktail sauce, and popped it into his mouth. "The fire's going."

"That's good," she answered.

"Anything else I can do?"

She looked around. "Would you like to finish setting the table? They should be here any minute."

Nate opened the box of silverware, counted out six of each utensil, and carried them into the dining room. He placed silver at each setting and lit the candles. Shaking out the match, he walked into the living room and threw it into the fire. Just as he did, there was a knock at the door, and without waiting for an answer, Samuel pushed it open. With a voice sounding like Santa Claus, he boomed, "Merry Christmas!"

"Merry Christmas to you!" Nate answered, smiling broadly and shaking hands with Samuel and both boys before finally turning to Sarah for a hug. "And how are you, my dear?"

Sarah smiled warmly at him. "Oh, fine. Merry Christmas!"

Nate took their coats, and Noelle came in from the kitchen.

"Merry Christmas!" she said, greeting each one of them with a hug. Asa just stood by the door and watched. She was lovelier than he remembered, and he could not look away. She finally made her way over to him and with her eyes, told him how well she remembered the intimacy they had known. She grabbed his hands and kissed him lightly on the cheek, lingering briefly and murmuring, "Merry Christmas." She stepped back, and he let go of her hands. He searched her eyes, his whole body aching.

Nate returned from hanging coats and eyed Samuel. "The usual?"

"Sounds good."

He turned to Sarah.

She smiled. "*My* usual, too, please."

Nate busied himself at the bar, and Isaac elbowed Asa. "What're you havin'?"

Asa elbowed him back. "Just a beer."

Isaac joined his parents at the bar, and Asa slipped into the kitchen.

"Need help?"

Noelle smiled warmly at him. "Oh, Asa, it's so good to see you." He instantly felt relieved. "How's school going? Do you like it? I can't believe how long it's been since I've seen you." She paused and studied him. "You look wonderful—thinner, though."

"You look wonderful too." He paused. "I've missed you."

Noelle's heart pounded. "I've missed you too—more than you know . . ." She hesitated. "Asa, I hope we have a chance to talk—" She was interrupted as Isaac pushed open the kitchen door.

He smiled and handed Asa a beer. Glancing around the kitchen, he saw that Noelle didn't have a drink. "Noelle, can I get something for you?"

Asa hoped she would say yes so that his brother would leave.

"No thanks, Isaac. I'm all set."

"Okay, well, if there's anything I can do . . ."

"Actually, would you like to take out this tray of shrimp cocktail?"

"Sure." Isaac set down his drink and picked up the tray. "I'll have to test one first," he said, winking at his brother. He offered the tray to Asa, who declined, wishing his brother would just hurry up and move on. Isaac pointed to his beer and eyed him. "That's mine," he warned, and carried the tray into the living room.

Asa took a sip of his beer and looked at Noelle. She was watching him. "I know what's going through your mind," she said with a smile.

"No, you don't," he teased, taking another sip.

She picked up a small platter with crisp apples slices around a wedge of cheddar and started to follow Isaac. Asa put his arm up to block her way.

"Do you want some?" she asked softly.

"Do I!" he murmured, leaning forward and softly kissing her neck. He quickly found her lips, and Noelle closed her eyes and felt a warm rush of heat surge through her body. *God, why do I always lose control when he is standing in front of me?* A sound came from the other side of the door, and she quickly stepped back, feeling her cheeks flush. She studied Asa's eyes and whispered, "I'm sorry . . ."

"For what?" he said, bewildered by her apology.

Isaac pushed open the door, and Asa moved away. Isaac reached for his drink and looked at his brother curiously.

"I have these snacks," Noelle sighed, "but everything else is just about ready." She paused. "Isaac, would you ask Nate to come carve the turkey?"

Asa quickly interjected, "I can carve the turkey." Immediately, though, he wanted to kick himself because he realized that, if he had said nothing, his brother would have left again and the moment alone might have been extended.

"Okay," Noelle said skeptically, handing him the worn wooden case that held the carving utensils. "Be careful, though," she warned, eyeing him. "It's very sharp."

Just then, Sarah came into the kitchen, too, followed by Nate and Samuel.

"How can I help?" Sarah asked.

Noelle smiled and opened the oven door. Nate stepped in and, sliding two oven mitts onto his hands, pulled the tremendous roasting pan out and set it down on the stove top. Everyone oohed and aahed over its contents, and Noelle pointed to a stack of ceramic hot plates and asked Isaac if he would please put them on the table. Then, as Nate carefully lifted the golden brown bird onto the cutting board, Noelle started to mix flour and water for gravy. Not knowing that Asa had offered to carve the turkey, Nate reached for the utensils, and, without a word, Asa relinquished them. He watched his father open a second bottle of chardonnay; he watched his mother open the oven and begin to take out hot bowls of sweet potatoes, stuffing, and string beans; he watched Isaac find another pair of pot holders and begin to help carry the dishes to the dining room. Everyone laughed and chatted busily—except Asa, who just stood there and felt oddly out of place. He looked around at the kitchen full of people and felt very much alone.

Nate started to carve the turkey and eyed the boys. "Who'd like a piece of skin?"

Asa half smiled, remembering all the times he and Isaac had stood by Nate's side when he was carving, waiting for him to offer the crisp juicy morsels that melted in their mouths. "That's the best part!" they had exclaimed, trying not to appear too impolite as they jostled for the biggest piece.

Isaac reappeared and smiled. "I'll force myself," he said. He popped a piece into his mouth, and Nate looked at Asa, who shook his head. "No thanks."

## 71

Only once during dinner did Noelle allow her eyes to meet Asa's. She was seated at one end of the table while he was at the far end, beside Nate. When it happened, everyone was occupied passing food, and Noelle could tell that Nate was involved in a conversation with Samuel, so no one noticed when she paused to look at Asa, and no one noticed when he looked up and caught her eye.

No one, that is, except Sarah, who had been chatting with Isaac but happened to look up and see the furtive, unspoken exchange of intimacy that smoldered between them. She glanced quickly from one to the other, startled and unsure. *It was nothing,* she assured herself. *How silly,* she chided herself. Noelle quickly averted her eyes and casually asked Isaac how school was going, and Sarah took a sip of her wine and tried to convince herself that she was mistaken.

After dinner, Asa helped clear the table. He tried to convince his mother to go in and enjoy the fire, that he would help Noelle clean up, but she would have none of it. So Asa silently dried dishes while Noelle and Sarah chatted, and all the while, he tried to think of another way to be alone with Noelle. Finally, he hung up the dish towel and held out dessert plates as Noelle placed the pies onto them. Sarah disappeared briefly to see if anyone wanted coffee.

Asa seized the moment. "Noelle, I need to see you alone," he said quietly.

"We are alone," she teased.

"Not like this." He paused. "You know what I mean."

She looked up and smiled. "Asa, I *do* know what you mean, and I would love to be alone with you—"

She was interrupted by Sarah pushing open the door again. "I guess everyone's having coffee. Asa, why don't you bring out the dessert?"

Asa clenched his jaw in frustration.

The fire crackled warmly as everyone relaxed. Isaac scraped his plate, set it on the coffee table, and leaned back on the couch. "I am absolutely stuffed," he said, stretching out his legs.

"I hope you're not too full to open your gift," Nate said, setting down his coffee and looking under the tree. When Annie died, the boys had stopped hanging their stockings on the mantel. Instead, Nate had started a new tradition of thoughtfully selecting a new book for each of the boys. In the beginning, he had given them such classics as *Mike Mulligan and His Steam Shovel* and *The Biggest Bear*. But before long, he was choosing chapter books like *Old Yeller* and *The Red Pony*. In recent years, the selection had become even more sophisticated. Nate pulled a neatly wrapped gift from under the tree and handed it to Isaac; then he turned to search for Asa's present. Isaac waited until Asa had his before he opened up one end and carefully slipped out a new hardcover. It was John Updike's latest effort, *Rabbit, Run*.

"Thanks, Uncle Nate," Isaac said. He held up the book to show his parents, and a magazine clipping fell from the book.

"You're welcome," Nate replied, smiling. "You're not going to believe this, but John Updike was at the Red Sox game we went to. In fact, he was sitting near us!" He paused. "I had no idea myself until I saw that essay in the *New Yorker*."

He nodded toward the floor, and Isaac picked up the article and read the headline out loud: " 'Hub Fans Bid Kid Adieu.' "

"I don't know if I would recognize him," Nate continued, "but in the essay he says he was sitting right behind the dugout!"

"I don't think I would have recognized him either," Samuel said, shaking his head, "but that's pretty neat."

"I hope you like the book," Nate added.

"Oh, I'm sure I will," Isaac replied.

All eyes turned to Asa, and he smiled nervously as he slipped his book from its wrapping. He turned it over to look at the cover, and his heart stopped. He stared at the familiar illustration of a boy standing near a tree. It was the same book he had picked up in Boston on the morning after the ball game. John Knowles's *A Separate Peace,* Asa now knew, was about the betrayal of a friendship. Asa's heart pounded—was Nate trying to tell him something?

"Th-thank you," he stammered, looking up and forcing a smile. He ran his hand over the cover, almost as if trying to wipe it away.

"You're welcome," he began. "I haven't read it, but I thought it looked like something you'd enjoy."

Asa held it up for his parents and Noelle to see and then feigned unfamiliarity by leafing through the pages.

Nate drew attention away from Asa as he cleared his throat. He had his hands behind his back, and he smiled mischievously as he approached Noelle. "I have one more gift," he said. "It's actually a surprise for everyone." He handed Noelle an elegantly wrapped scroll-shaped package. Noelle looked up at him questioningly and hesitated before slowly untying the ribbon. As she did, the delicate tissue paper fell away, and a festive Christmas stocking unfurled in her lap. The bottom of the stocking was made of soft red felt, and the top, which was folded over, was pure white.

## 72

Noelle's heart raced. She looked at Nate and tried to convey her startled surprise—her desire for him to go no further—but Nate was not looking at her. He was looking at the hooks on the mantel. "It's definitely been a while since a stocking has hung on this mantel," he began, "and we don't yet know what name will be embroidered on this one but . . ." He turned around and smiled.

Sarah drew in an astonished breath, realizing what he was trying to say. "Oh, my! Oh, how wonderful!" She turned to Noelle and hugged her. "I'm so happy for you! How're you feeling? When are you due?" Sarah was absolutely beaming, as if the news were her own, and she stood to give Nate a hug. "Congratulations!" she said, taking his hands.

Nate smiled, and Samuel caught on too. He stood to shake Nate's hand and slapped him on the back.

"Hot damn!" Samuel said. "You see, I told you miracles happen!"

Isaac also stood. "That's such good news!"

Noelle glanced quickly at Asa. His face had turned ashen,

and he was staring into the fire. *This isn't the way it's supposed to be,* she thought. *This isn't the way I wanted it to be.* Her heart reached out to him, but he refused to look at her.

Instead he stared blindly at the flames as a rushing fury of jealousy and disbelief swept through him. *Did I really think she didn't sleep with him? Who was I fooling? Only myself!* He could not bring himself to look at her. His hands were trembling. *I have been such a fool. I should tell them everything. How would that make her feel? Why should I suffer this madness and misery alone? Who the hell cares what happens now? It's over. It's just over.* Asa's vision was blurry with pent-up rage.

It seemed like an eternity, but it was only seconds before Sarah's voice penetrated the darkness that had enveloped him and brought him to his senses. "Asa, isn't this good news?"

Asa looked up and quickly stood to shake Nate's hand. "Congratulations," he said with a nod.

Nate smiled gently and thanked him. Asa obediently turned to Noelle, and she searched his eyes, wanting to take him in her arms and explain everything, but it was not the time or place. There was nothing she could do. Asa hugged her stiffly and turned away. He leaned against the mantel and silently watched Nate hang the new Christmas stocking on the hook that had been his, and then he looked at Noelle once more. This time the look on Asa's face was one she had never seen before; it was almost as if he were wearing a mask. The eyes that had once smoldered with tender desire now burned with unforgiving bitterness, and both of their hearts shattered.

## ❧ 73 ❧

Winter had a firm grip on the New Hampshire countryside when Asa returned to school. The campus was blanketed in deep snow that drifted across the walkways. The bare trees moaned and shivered in the darkness, and the ice on the river boomed and echoed in the night. The icy fingers of winter also gripped Asa's heart.

After Christmas Eve, he had not seen Noelle again. The opportunity to be alone, if only to talk, had never come. Even if it had, Asa had nothing to say, and whatever *she* might say, he had no interest in hearing. In his mind, there was no room in her life now for a relationship with him, and the hope he had clung to had been crushed.

Asa's classmates noticed a change in the introverted student from Boston. He began to turn up at parties, drank excessively and, more than once, was seen kneeling in a snowbank after drinking too much. His grades continued their free fall as well, but Asa no longer cared—about his grades, his future, or his well-being. He stopped running and frequently drank to obliv-

220 / *Nan Rossiter*

ion. Gin, as was tradition—or so he told himself—was the poison of choice, and he drank it straight out of the bottle.

Asa didn't need a party to drink either. By February, he was barely making it to class. On the second Tuesday in February, Asa woke with a pounding head and realized he had already missed his first class, not to mention breakfast. He looked at the empty bottle on his desk and decided if he went into town, he could grab breakfast at the diner and then replenish his supply. He reached for a bottle of aspirin, shook it, and realized he needed that too. He didn't bother to shower; he just pulled on his jeans and hiking boots, which smelled faintly of vomit, threw a jacket on over his T-shirt, and trudged out into the snow.

It was another raw, gray New England day, and by the time Asa pulled open the door of the diner, he was frozen. He was grateful to just sit at the counter and wrap his hands around a steaming cup of coffee. He ordered eggs and bacon, and as he waited, he looked around and noticed that the diner was decorated with red cardboard hearts. He strained his eyes to see the date on the calendar behind the coffee pot: February 14.

*It figures.* He shook his head. He discovered that his thoughts were constantly lined with bitter sarcasm now, there was no escaping it. He thought of Noelle and how she might look—surely she was showing. Maybe by now, Nate wasn't getting any satisfaction either. It served him right, the son of a bitch.

The cook in back had the radio playing, and the waitress at the counter called for him to turn it up, saying, "I love this song!" She sang along softly with Elvis as she wiped down the counter and then smiled at Asa. "This song's number one, you know." She continued to wipe and sing the sad song about being lonesome, and Asa cradled his hands around the warm cup and closed his eyes.

A truck driver at the other end of the counter caught her hand as she walked by and, with a wink, said, "As a matter of fact, I am." She laughed and refilled his cup. Slowly but steadily, Asa's mood deteriorated further. He picked at his food, paid his bill, and finally left the diner, heading down the street to the package store.

The owner of the store eyed him with mild concern as he put the bottle in a bag. He wondered what was going on with this kid. This was the second time this week. Asa avoided his eyes as he paid, mumbled a "thank you," and pushed open the door. He had bought aspirin, and as he stepped out onto the street, he opened the bottle of pills and the bottle of gin, washed one down with the other, and trudged through town toward the river.

## 74

There wasn't much traffic on Ledyard Bridge that morning. Asa stood on the eastern bank of the Connecticut River and looked across to Vermont. The ice flows crept along, deceptively promising safe passage by foot. Asa watched and knew better. He wandered over to an old tree stump and sat down, pulled up the collar of his jacket, and opened the gin bottle again. He drank without removing the paper bag and didn't care if he looked like a derelict—no one was watching, and no one cared anyway.

He chipped at the frozen stump and remembered the story he had once heard about Dartmouth student John Ledyard, for whom the bridge was named. According to local history, in 1773, Ledyard had dropped out of Dartmouth to become an adventurer. He had cut down a tree, carved a dugout canoe, and set off down the Connecticut River to explore the world. The idea intrigued Asa, and he took another long swig and wondered if the stump on which he sat was the remains of that tree.

The periphery of Asa's vision grew darker as he drank. Tears burned at his eyes, and he ran his hand through his hair in an-guished frustration. He didn't want to remember, but the mem-ories kept flooding back into his mind. He had convinced himself that drinking helped him forget, but today as he stared at the icy river, the alcohol only seemed to intensify the images that played through his mind. In a blur of confusion, the images flashed before his eyes like scenes from a movie that had no script, a movie in which he had played a part but now only watched from outside. . . .

Noelle painting the house, laughing, smiling at him, reciting the books of the Bible. Without realizing it, Asa murmured, "Genesis . . . Exodus . . . Leviticus . . ." Then a dark choir loft, a figure hovering over her. Nate putting his arms around her, kissing her neck, soft curtains billowing in the summer breeze, candles flickering, Noelle lying beside him. It was so real that his hand reached out to stroke her smooth skin. Firelight dancing on the wall, her body intertwined with his, her hair falling softly around his face . . . Sarah sitting alone in the dawn light . . . Martha watching him go, waiting for him, waiting . . . standing on the beach in the darkness, alone, praying . . . "Please come," he whispered out loud. "Please come." It's not because I don't love you . . . "Please come . . ." Asa squeezed his eyes shut and opened them again. Nate standing by the mantel, smiling. Turning away, Noelle searching his eyes, pleading, and then darkness all around him . . .

Asa got up suddenly and lurched toward the bridge. The road swayed before him, and he held on to the railing, lunging forward and stumbling out to the very center of the bridge. He looked down at the dark ice gliding slowly below him and shiv-ered uncontrollably. Taking the bottle from the bag, he held it up in a toast and slurred incoherently, "Sure as the stars return again after they merge in the light"—he paused, shook the bot-tle, and tipped the last drops back into his throat and continued—"death is as great as life . . ." Asa leaned precariously over the railing and shouted at the wind, "Ha, maybe death *is* better than life!" His hands shook from the cold, and the bottle slipped from his grasp. Asa watched it spiral downward and shatter across the ice, echoing like a gunshot, and then he crumpled to the ground and sobbed.

# ❧ 75 ❧

Asa did not remember the pickup truck that pulled up next to him. He did not remember the blond-haired farmer's son who steadied him and guided him to the passenger side of his truck. He did not remember the blanket that the boy threw on top of him or the conversation the boy had with a student outside the dorm. Asa had no recollection of the two boys bearing his weight and stealing through a side door into the dorm. The only thing he remembered was being asked for his key and then swaying in the doorway.

Asa shook his head and tried to focus. He had to stop the room from spinning. He was tired of the darkness around the edges of everything he looked at. He had to act normal. He had to stand up straight and speak clearly, because for some reason, his father was standing by the window in his room.

Asa leaned against the door and glanced around. He wished he had taken time to straighten up a bit. He cleared his throat. "Hey, Dad, what are you doing here?" He spoke slowly and tried to enunciate each word, which only made his slurred speech more pronounced.

Samuel shook his head. "I wouldn't have believed it if I hadn't seen it for myself. Asa, what the hell are you doing?"

Asa immediately became defensive. "What do you mean, what am *I* doing?" Suddenly, a wave of nausea swept over him, and he backed out of the room and stumbled down the hall to the lavatory. Samuel followed him and waited. When he was convinced that Asa had nothing left in his stomach, he turned on the hot water in one of the showers and told him to strip off his clothes and get in. Asa obeyed and Samuel took the pile of soiled clothes back to his son's room. He located shampoo, soap and a washcloth, moderately clean clothes, toothpaste, and a toothbrush.

While Asa slept, Samuel straightened up the room. He gathered up the empty bottles and trash and threw them away; he found the laundry room and put in a load; and while he waited for the clothes to dry, he reread the letter from the dean that had requested parental intervention. The letter stated that Asa had not responded to requests for a meeting; he was currently failing all of his classes; he had not adjusted to responsible independent living; and he would be thrown out of school if he did not turn his behavior and grades around. Samuel sighed, retrieved the laundered clothes, and started to fold them. He watched Asa sleeping restlessly and thought of the many nights he had leaned against the doorway of his sons' bedroom, watching them sleep. He pictured the shaft of light from the hallway that had illuminated their room, and he remembered the feeling of awe and wonder as he had looked at their slight figures, their summer sheets kicked off, their stuffed bears tucked tightly under their arms. He remembered the many nights he had leaned down to kiss their wispy blond hair and breathe in the sweet, lovely scent of boyish innocence, and the many nights he had stood by as they lay dreaming and wondered what their futures held; and he remembered the many nights he had knelt by their beds and prayed, thanking God for gifts so amazing and asking Him to look after them, to hold them close, when he could not.

Samuel prayed that same prayer now.

Finally, convinced that Asa would continue sleeping, he slipped out of the room again, drove to town, found a deli that was getting ready to close, and bought two sandwiches and two cups of coffee. When he returned, Asa was sitting on the edge of his bed, holding his head in his hands.

He looked up sheepishly. "I'm sorry, Dad."

Samuel handed him one of the steaming cups and pulled a chair up closer to the bed. Then he handed the letter to him. Asa glanced at it and tried to figure out what to say. He looked up, and Samuel searched his son's eyes for an explanation, but Asa just looked away. More than anything, he wanted to explain; he wished he could tell his father everything. But the truth was certainly beyond forgiveness—the truth would, without a doubt, change his relationship with his father forever.

Asa took a sip of the coffee and almost burned his tongue. He shook his head, looked at the letter again, and stole an eleventh-hour explanation from the words on the page. *Foolishness, lack of responsibility,* and *trouble adjusting* were some of the words that spilled from his mouth. He listened to his father's patient reply and nodded at every suggestion to not forget his upbringing, to go to church, to remember that God was with him, no matter where he was or what he did. At these words, Asa stared at his cup. *Does Dad somehow know? Why would he say "no matter what I did"?* He glanced up and tried to read his father's face, but it revealed nothing but concern. Asa apologized again and promised to buckle down.

They ate the sandwiches in silence until Samuel glanced at his watch and stood to go. He reached for his coat, said he would call the dean in the morning, and insisted that Asa go see him, too, first thing. Then he wrapped his son in a hug and told him that he loved him. Asa nodded. "Love you, too, Dad." When the door had closed, Asa collapsed on his bed and whispered, "Oh, God, please help me get over her. . . ."

## 76

As winter finally gave way to warm spring days, Noelle gently pushed back on the tiny foot that slid across the inside of her swollen belly. She smiled when she felt the steady small palpitations that her doctor said were hiccups. And, after breathing in the scent of her body, she bought and tucked away a tiny blue outfit, convinced that the deep musky scent she smelled was not her own.

At Nate's insistence, she had stopped working and now found that she had too much time on her hands—too much time to think, too much time to wonder. *Have I made the right decision?* She longed to see Asa, just to know how he was doing and if he had forgiven her. She stood at the kitchen window and watched a small troupe of red-breasted sentinels hopping across her yard, pausing every so often to cock their heads and listen to the earth. She watched the late-afternoon sun setting behind the trees and thought about the passage of time. She remembered the way the sky had looked on that agonizing night in September, now it seemed so very long ago. Noelle watched the sun sink below the horizon and wondered if Asa had received her letters. She had written so many, apologizing and asking him to find some reason to stop by when he was home. But he had not come by; he hadn't even come home. Offhandedly, Noelle had asked Sarah how he was and why he hadn't come home for Easter. Sarah had said he was fine, that he'd simply decided to stay at school. In fact, he'd even found a summer job at the library in Hanover. Noelle had nodded, trying to hide her dismay.

She had no way of knowing how Asa was managing, no way of knowing how he felt or if he had forgiven her. She had no way of reaching him, of telling him all the things she wanted to say, and now more than ever, she worried that she would never have the chance. She gripped the kitchen counter and whispered, "Oh, God, how is he?"

## 77

*One more exam,* Asa thought as he laced up his running shoes. It was only 5:30, but the sun was already peeking over the horizon. He slipped quietly out of the dorm and stretched his legs. The birds called sleepily and tentatively from the trees that lined the campus. Asa wondered if the same early riser began the chorus every morning or if they competed to see who would be first to rouse the others? He pictured a chickadee, all puffed up and sound asleep. Did she, when she heard a cardinal's call, open one eye and blink? Did she stretch her wings and make a sound? Or did she close her eyes again and enjoy a few more minutes of rest? Asa smiled at the thought and began to run toward town.

His exam was not until 9:30, and he was confident he would do well. He and his classmates would have two hours to write two essays comparing the works of Hemingway and Fitzgerald. The reading for the class had been demanding: F. Scott's *The Great Gatsby* and *Tender Is the Night,* and Hemingway's *For Whom the Bell Tolls* and *The Sun Also Rises.* Asa had enjoyed every word written by the two authors—the drinking, the romance, the insanity. He even credited the novels with his own survival.

After his father's unexpected visit, Asa had kept his promise. He had spoken with the dean, apologized again, and expressed his desire to continue his studies. He had resumed his running regiment, spent long nights catching up on missed assignments, and, in spite of himself, even made a few friends. But he forbade himself from thinking about Noelle. The memories still came, unbidden, and washed over him with the force of a riptide, but Asa slowly learned to push them back and think of other things.

That morning, however, his mind was clear, and he pushed himself to run farther and farther. He headed for the bridge and over into Vermont, then followed the river and the long winding stretch of farmland. He ran along a quiet country road and watched a blond-haired boy attaching a plow to an old John Deere tractor. A dog barked and the boy looked up. Asa waved and the boy waved back.

When he returned to campus, Asa stretched in front of the student center. Beads of perspiration trickled down along his hairline while he waited for the building to open. When it did, he went in, looked through the glass window of his mailbox, and immediately recognized the familiar pale stationery. He slipped the envelope out and ran his hand over the elegant handwriting. A bead of moisture fell onto the ink and created a blue puddle. Asa walked slowly back to his room, pulled a dusty shoe box from under his bed, lifted off the top, dropped the letter onto a pile of unopened envelopes, replaced the top, and pushed the box back under the bed. Then he reached for his towel.

# ❧ 78 ❧

The sky was cobalt blue, with feathery wisps of white floating by, when Noelle drove out to the Cape on that June morning. Nate had planned to open up the house over Memorial Day weekend, but he had been too busy with work, so the following week, Noelle decided to go out to the Cape alone. She pulled slowly up the driveway and admired the freshly painted siding. She pictured Asa sitting on the ladder, his tattered Red Sox hat turned backward. *Oh, how she missed him.* She knew that coming back here would remind her of Asa, but that was the reason she had come—she *wanted* to remember.

She unlocked the front door and pushed it open. She felt the baby move and supported the bottom of her belly with her hand. The house had been closed up since Christmas, and it smelled of must and ashes. She opened the blinds and windows as she made her way through the rooms. There were no blinds in the kitchen, though, and the summer sun filled it with light. Noelle reached over the sink to push the window up. As she turned the latch, she felt a sharp pain deep in her belly. She winced and caught her breath and then bent over in agony. She made her way slowly out to the porch to sit down. *Maybe Nate was right—maybe I shouldn't have come alone.* She struggled to uncover a chair, eased into it, and tried to take slow, deep breaths. The pain finally subsided, and she promised herself that she would take it easy.

Leaning back in the chair, she looked at the doorway into the kitchen and pictured Asa standing there. She closed her eyes and smelled the summer rain and the scent of his body. She put her hands over her swollen belly and ran her fingers around in slow, rhythmic circles. The baby responded by pushing one foot out and creating a small lump in the roundness. Noelle listened to the distant waves, breathed in the ocean air, and was filled with contentment.

She dozed off but woke with a start when she heard a cardinal calling. Easing herself from the chair, she pushed open the screen door and stepped out into the yard to see if she could spot him. She glanced at the empty feeder and wondered if there was any seed left in the barrel. She made a mental note to buy some when she went to the store later. Then, out of the corner of her eye, she caught a flash of scarlet. Noelle looked up as a male cardinal flew to a branch above her head. Just as suddenly, though, her eyes were drawn away from him. There was something out of place—something was hanging from one of the lower branches. *Oh, no!* She stared in disbelief and moved closer, trying to grasp the sadness of what she saw.

A piece of thin string was tangled around a limb, and hanging upside down from the other end was a motionless female cardinal, the string tangled around her leg. *How did this happen? How had she become so completely ensnared? Had she been attracted to the string for her nest?* The image of the poor bird's struggle played through her mind, and she imagined her frantic efforts to free herself. *Oh, how she must have tried to escape—how she must have suffered!* Tears filled Noelle's eyes while the male cardinal continued to call, fluttering from limb to limb and cocking his head to look at Noelle. It was almost as if he were asking her to help his lifelong mate. "Oh, God," she cried out. "How did this happen? Where were you when she was trying to free herself? Why weren't you watching?" Hot, angry tears spilled down her cheeks.

Noelle hurried into the house and found the items she would need. With scissors, she cut the string from the branch and gently laid the tawny red bird on the grass. In her grief, it didn't occur to her to simply cut the string away; instead, she immediately became intent on untying it. Painstakingly, and with tears in her eyes, she worked away at the merciless knot until it finally yielded to her efforts and the little bird's lifeless body was free. Noelle placed the cardinal on a soft towel in a shoe box and gently stroked her beautiful feathers. Then she found a shady spot beneath the lilac bush and dug a small hole. The whole time she worked, the male cardinal perched at the top of a lilac bloom and watched, still calling and cocking his head.

When she had covered up the hole, Noelle sat on the grass and, through a blur of tears, looked up at the brokenhearted mate and whispered, "I'm so sorry."

The Bourne Bridge loomed majestically ahead. Asa looked out over the canal and remembered the anticipation he had felt when he had crossed the bridge last September; he recalled how the evening sun had cast its rosy light across the treetops, and he shook his head. So much had happened since then.

Samuel glanced over. "Have you ever seen such a blue sky?"

Asa smiled. He rolled down his window and breathed in the ocean air.

"I appreciate the ride, Dad," he said. "I hope you don't mind if I don't hang around." He paused. He didn't want to linger any longer than was necessary, he didn't want to remember. "It's a long drive, you know," he said, adding, "I hope the truck starts." After Asa had presented a respectable report card, he had convinced his parents that he would need his truck if he was going to stay in New Hampshire for the summer. Even though the Howe Library was right on West Wheelock Street and he could walk to his new job there, he wanted to have the truck so he could explore the countryside and get away. He had bought a used backpack, and he planned to hike in the White Mountains, maybe even hike part of the Appalachian Trail.

When they reached the house, Asa climbed out and walked around to where he had left the truck. It was dusty and covered with leaves, but it sputtered to life on the second try, and while it was warming up, he walked around back to see where his parents had buried Martha. He knelt down and pulled away some weeds from the fresh earth and ran his hand over the large smooth stone marker that his father had found along the water's edge. The air was fragrant with the heady sweet smell of lilacs, and tears welled up in Asa's eyes. "Hello, ole girl," he whispered.

Samuel came up behind him and laid his hand on Asa's shoulder. "She was a good pal, and she definitely loved *you* best. She knew she had to keep her eye on you. In fact, without her, you might not even be here." Asa smiled, nodding through his tears, and remembered the frightening riptide that had swept him away from shore when he was a boy. Martha had barked frantically before jumping in and swimming out to him. Asa had clung to her, and she had instinctively swam with the current, bringing him safely back to shore.

Asa stood up and wiped his eyes. Samuel reached into his pocket, took out his wallet, and handed Asa several crisp bills. "This is for gas and to hold you over until your first paycheck. Call if you need more." Asa reached out to shake his father's hand, and Samuel smiled and pulled him into a hug. "We'll miss you, you know."

"I'll miss you, too, Dad."

"Behave."

"I will," Asa said with a half-smile.

## 80

Asa turned the truck onto Route 6 and pulled into the first gas station he came to. An attendant filled up the truck and told Asa he needed a quart of oil. Asa nodded, and while the attendant took care of it, he walked over to the soda machine and dropped in a quarter. He tilted a frosty bottle of Dr Pepper into the metal slot, popped off the cap, and took a sip. He handed the attendant one of the bills his father had given him, took his change, climbed into the truck, and pulled back onto Route 6 West. As he turned onto the familiar rotary, he leaned across the seat to unroll the window and pictured Martha leaning out as far as she could with her ears flapping in the breeze. Asa eased over to the right and onto the highway entrance, and as he did, he glanced to his left and caught the taillights of a turquoise Bel Air turning off the rotary and heading toward Orleans. Asa squinted at the plate. It was definitely from Massachusetts, but he couldn't make out the numbers, and then it was gone. Asa slowed down to a crawl, and the car that had been behind him drove by, beeping its horn, but Asa just stared straight ahead, his knuckles white from gripping the steering wheel, his heart pounding.

Noelle returned to Boston a few days later, tan and refreshed. Nate pulled her into his arms and said she looked beautiful. He stroked her belly and murmured, "How is *he?*"

"What do you mean, *he?*"

"Just a guess," he said with a quiet smile. "What shall we call him?"

Noelle closed her eyes. "You know . . ."

"Are you sure?"

"Yes." She paused. "I'm sure."

She tried to pull away, but Nate wasn't ready to let go. "I've missed you."

"I've missed you too," she whispered, blinking back tears.

The Howe Library was established in 1900 when Emily Howe donated her family home to the town of Hanover, praying that "this library may prove a blessing to this community to the remotest generation." The house had originally been commissioned by Eleazar Wheelock, founder and president of Dartmouth College, and was built in 1773 by a journeyman carpenter named Hezekiah Davenport. "The Wheelock Mansion," as it was called, was originally a two-story structure with a gambrel roof and four chimneys.

Asa walked along the shady tree-lined street and looked up at the historic old structure. It was only his second day at the library, but he already felt as if he knew as much about the building as the town's historian. From the librarian, Mrs. Draper, he had learned that the original building had been bought and moved to its present address at West Wheelock Street in 1838. He also knew that the building had gone through several drastic renovations; that the Howe family did not begin residing there until 1851; and that it was not until 1888 or so that the Widow Howe, Emily's mother, actually purchased the house.

Asa pulled open the heavy door and immediately felt at home. He loved the dusty smell of old books and papers. He smiled at the librarian, found the ancient wooden book cart, and wheeled it along the fiction aisles, looking for *Alcott, Louisa May,* and pictured the young girl who must have just finished *Little Women.* He continued on, slipped a slim volume of Edgar Allan Poe off the shelf for himself, and then began to look for Steinbeck—someone had just returned the tome *East of Eden.* Asa put it back in its place between *Cannery Row* and *Of Mice and Men* and continued on, pushing the cart around the corner. He looked up and saw a young woman about his age sitting at a table by the window. She was slender, and her blond hair was pulled back in a ponytail. Her glasses were perched on the end of her nose, and she had a mountain of books and papers in front of her. Asa wondered what she was working on.

## ❧ 83 ❧

It was unusually cool for the first day of summer. Noelle clutched the ticket in her hand and waited impatiently for the bus to pull in. Nate had said he would be working late, but that still didn't allow much time for what she needed to do. She wondered for the hundredth time if she should have driven. *No, I made the right choice.* Nate would surely notice the spike in miles on her odometer, and it would be easier for her to ride than drive. She just prayed that she didn't have another recurrence of pain. *Oh, God, I wish the bus would get here. . . .*

## ❧ 84 ❧

Asa glanced at the calendar and could not believe it was already the first day of summer. He went into the library early. It didn't take long to shelve the few books that had been returned. He leaned on his cart and wondered how he would stay busy. He was definitely going to have to find a second job—one that would actually keep him busy. Finally, he decided to ask Mrs. Draper if he might come back later in the afternoon. She peered at him over her glasses, looked around the quiet library, and nodded.

## ≈ 85 ≈

Noelle stared out the window as the bus crossed into New Hampshire. Raindrops streamed across the glass, chasing each other, and she wished she had thought to bring an umbrella. She stroked her belly to calm herself, and the familiar little foot responded, pushing out. She felt a tightening, dull pain, but it was not nearly as bad as before. Her doctor had assured her it was only false labor and not to worry. She had a little over a week before her due date. She looked out at the green hills and smiled as her hand followed the little bulge that swept across her belly.

## ❧ 86 ❧

Asa pushed open the library door and realized it was sprinkling. He paused to watch the young woman from the day before hurrying up the walk. Her arms were full of books, and he held the door for her. She nodded and thanked him. He nodded back and wondered if he should stay. He glanced at the sky—no, he would go. While he was on his run that morning, he had seen the farmer's son hooking up the baler, and he was certain they could use a hand getting in the hay before it rained. . . .

## 87

Noelle paused to glance from the piece of paper in her hand to the street sign marking the intersection of West Wheelock and South Main. The rain had let up, but it was still gray and cool. She pulled her sweater snugly around her body, as best she could, and turned toward the library. She felt her heart race, and she tried to catch her breath.

## 88

The rusty green and yellow tractor slowed down as Asa walked across the field. One of the farmer's sons strained to throw a heavy bale to his younger brother and then paused to look up.

"Need a hand?" Asa shouted, motioning with his arms.

The farmer looked at the threatening sky and nodded. Asa fell in opposite the older son, and they both worked the field. The boys looked at him curiously, and the older son recognized him as the runner ... but thought he knew him from somewhere else too. The bales were heavy, and the twine burned Asa's hands. He wished he had gloves, but when he looked at the two boys, he noticed that they didn't have any either; he would just have to rough it.

# 89

Noelle tentatively pulled open the heavy door. The librarian and the young woman at the table both looked up. Noelle smiled and walked over to the desk.

"Good morning," the librarian said, taking in Noelle's full form.

"Good morning," Noelle replied quietly. "I am looking for Asa Coleman."

The woman at the table watched her curiously, wondering who this lady was and what connection she had to the young man who worked here.

The librarian was having the same thought as she answered, "He's not here right now, but he said he would be back this afternoon."

Noelle paused and looked at the ancient Seth Thomas clock hanging above the desk. It was already 12:10. She would only be able to stay until 2:30. "Would it be all right if I waited? I'm a friend from out of town, and I was hoping to surprise him."

"Yes, of course. Please make yourself comfortable," she replied, nodding to Noelle.

## ❧ 90 ❧

Asa lifted the last bale onto the rickety metal conveyor and watched it rattle up to the hayloft. He turned around and saw a woman come into the barn and set down a jug of iced tea, glasses, and a plate of sandwiches. Asa had learned the boys' names earlier; Seth was the older son, named after his father, and Ethan was the younger boy. Now Asa introduced himself to Mrs. Asher, and she smiled warmly as she poured a large glass of sweet tea for each of them.

## 91

The only sound in the library was the steady, quiet clicking of the hands on the old clock. Noelle had taken a book from the book cart and settled into the worn Queen Anne's chair by the window, but she could not keep her mind on the words. Instead, her eyes were drawn to the relentlessly swinging pendulum that was stealing away anxious minutes. Silently, she prayed that Asa would come through the door. Finally, after almost two hours, she got up and asked the librarian for a piece of paper. The librarian opened her drawer, slipped out an ivory sheet with the library's letterhead at the top, and handed it, along with an envelope, to Noelle. Noelle thanked her and sat back down.

## 92

"You must be thirsty," Mrs. Asher said. "It's not easy work."

Asa rubbed his palms together and felt the new blisters stinging.

"No, it isn't. But it's good exercise."

Mr. Asher came up behind him. "Well, anytime you need some exercise, you're welcome here!"

"Please, have a sandwich." Mrs. Asher held the plate out. Asa glanced at his watch and couldn't believe the time.

"I really have to go," he said.

"Well, take it with you, then."

"Okay." Asa took a sandwich from the plate and put it on a napkin. "Thank you."

"Thank *you*. Lunch is the least we can do," Mr. Asher said, reaching for his wallet. "We can't give you much money. . . ."

Asa put up his hand. "I don't want to be paid—it was fun."

## 93

Tears welled up in Noelle's eyes as she wrote. She had not wanted Asa to find out this way. She had wanted to be able to tell him in person, to see his face—then she would know what to do. She chose her words carefully, just as she had rehearsed them so many times in her head. She folded the letter and slipped it into the envelope. On the outside, she wrote his name and then she glanced at the clock—it was 2:35. Noelle shook her head, took the letter out, and read it again. She looked at the door. *Why didn't he come?* Slowly, she stood up and walked toward the desk. She winced in pain and clutched the letter more tightly.

## 94

Asa shook hands with everyone before walking toward the barn door. He looked back. "When's second cutting?"

Mr. Asher smiled. " 'Bout a month—*if* your hands have recovered . . ."

"Sounds good—see you then!"

"Thanks again, son."

The boys looked down from the loft. "See you, Asa."

Asa waved and walked out into the rain.

## 95

The librarian looked up and saw the envelope in Noelle's hand. "I thought he would be back by now," she began. "Would you like me to give that to him?"

Noelle looked down at the name on the envelope. *Oh, Asa, where are you?*

Her hands were shaking as she put the book she had tried to read back on the cart. She glanced at the envelope again. "No. Thank you, though. You needn't even say I was here. I'll see him soon."

The librarian looked surprised as she studied Noelle's pale face. "Are you sure?"

"Yes." Noelle paused. "I'm sure."

Her trembling hands slipped the envelope into the book she had brought from home to give to Asa. She slipped the book back into her bag, and then she pushed open the door and stepped outside. Rain had started to fall again, and the drops blended with the tears on her cheeks.

## 96

"Is your name Asa?"

Asa turned to look at the young woman who had just passed him. He studied her face and tried to place her. Her eyes were a pretty hazel, and she had a smattering of freckles across the bridge of her nose. She had the hood of her jacket up, and at first he didn't recognize her without her glasses.

"Yes," he answered.

"I thought so," she began, "because I was at the library earlier, and there was someone looking for you."

Asa looked puzzled. "Looking for *me*?"

"Yes, I'm quite sure. I don't know if she's still there, but she waited a long time. She is . . ." the girl paused. "What I mean is, *I think* she is expecting."

Asa ran the rest of the way to the library. Mrs. Draper was locking the door as he came up the walk. "The library closes at three on Wednesdays," she said, putting up her umbrella and walking away. On the sidewalk in front of the library, Asa stood with his hands hanging at his sides and looked up at the falling rain. . . .

## ❦ 97 ❦

*If I can just make it to the car . . . Please let me make it to the car,* Noelle pleaded silently after finally arriving back in Boston. The pain deep in her belly was excruciating, and the concerned faces of passersby began to blend together. She saw her car in the parking lot where she had left it, and cradling her belly, she tried desperately to walk with some measure of normalcy. A sudden, shocking pain exploded inside of her abdomen, and she cried out as she fell forward. Nearby, a gentleman saw what was happening and rushed to catch her. Noelle collapsed onto the sidewalk and lay still, trying to focus. She looked up at the clouds and listened to the worried voices all around her. She noticed a patch of blue, the voices fading in and out. The summer sky was there all the time . . . the sweet summer sky. She closed her eyes and listened. The voices were quiet now, but there was another sound, faint at first . . . more clearly now . . . Yes, she was certain—a cardinal was calling. . . .

# ～ 98 ～

Nate heard the screaming siren pierce the normal sounds of evening traffic. It seemed to draw closer, and as he walked across Dewey Square, he paused to watch the commotion. A crowd had gathered, and the siren stopped abruptly as an ambulance pulled up in front of the bus station. Nate wondered what had happened and silently said a prayer, as he always did, for whoever it was who needed help. After several minutes, the crowd parted again and the ambulance pulled away, its lights flashing across the sky, the unsettling sound of its siren fading into the night.

When Nate pulled into the driveway of the old Victorian, he wondered where Noelle could be. He opened the car door, and even before he reached the back steps, he heard the telephone in the kitchen ringing impatiently. He hurriedly opened the door to answer it, and as he did, his hands started to shake. . . . The screaming siren, the impatient ringing, the voice on the other end all echoed through his mind.

## 99

The emergency room was swarming with activity as Nate frantically pressed the receptionist for information. A nursing friend of Noelle's looked up and recognized Nate. She quickly found Noelle's paperwork and began to explain. "They are wheeling her into surgery right now. . . ." But all Nate heard was *surgery* as he ran the length of the corridor, his heart pounding painfully in his chest. A second nurse put out her arm as he rushed toward the moving gurney, but he pushed past her and reached for Noelle's hand.

Noelle's eyes were closed, but she opened them when she felt his touch. "Oh, Nate," she murmured weakly, "I'm sorry . . . I'm so sorry. . . ." She seemed to drift in and out of consciousness. Nate pressed her hand to his lips as tears streamed down his cheeks. He held her hand as long as they would let him, even as the sea of worried voices threatened to drown him. *She has lost too much blood. . . . The baby is in distress. . . . Oh, God, get her in there. I don't know if we can save them. Sir, you must let go. . . .*

Asa looked up at the panes of glass and counted them again. Six across, eight up: forty-eight panes in the bottom and another forty in the top—eighty-eight panes in one set of windows; he thought of all the times he had counted these panes while sitting in the pew next to his brother, longing to be on the other side of them. He remembered how the minister had once asked them, during children's time, to think of something for which they were thankful, and Asa had said that he was thankful that it wasn't his job to keep all of those windows clean. The congregation had chuckled. Asa wished he could return to the innocence of that day.

They were beautiful windows, he thought, especially when the late-day sun filtered in, as it did now, causing the sanctuary to glow with an ethereal light. Isaac arrived late and slipped quietly into the pew beside him. The two boys sat a few rows behind their parents, who were seated in front with Nate. They stood for the last hymn, and Asa looked at Nate, who was bowed in sorrow, his shoulders sagging with grief. He looked at his parents standing beside Nate, bearing him up, and he looked out the window. *I loved her too. I loved her, and no one knows. No one will ever know how much I miss her.* He gripped the smooth wooden pew in front of him. *No one will ever say, "Asa, we are so sorry for your loss. We know how much she meant to you."* Asa stared at the wooden casket. *No one will ever know that I meant something to you and that you loved me.*

He looked out the window and listened to the words of the hymn. *When I tread the verge of Jordan . . . bid my anxious fears subside . . . death of death and hell's destruction . . . land me safe on Canaan's side.* He listened to the regal sound of a trumpet. *Songs of praises . . . songs of praises . . . I will ever give to thee.* Tears streamed down his cheeks as he whispered, "I will *never* give to thee. . . ."

*You . . . You have punished us all—guilty and innocent alike—and this is how it ends. She will never hold her child, and he . . . he will never know his mother. And I . . . I will never have the chance to tell her all the things I meant to say. Never again will I praise You. . . .*

The service ended, and the baby, cradled in Sarah's arms, cried out. Nate took the tiny bundle from her and walked slowly up to the front. He ran his fingers lightly over the smooth mahogany wood and bowed his head. Then he turned and slowly made his way up the aisle.

# Part III

*Stand at the crossroads, and look, and ask for the ancient paths,
where the good way lies; and walk in it.*

—Jeremiah 6:16

# 101

Asa closed *The Fountainhead* on his lap and leaned back in his chair. Then he hesitated, opened it to the last page, and read the last passage again, about the young college graduate wondering if life was worth living.

Asa closed the book, ran his hand over the cover, and thought about Ayn Rand's words. He watched the clear water rushing over the rocks; he knew what it was like to not feel inspired . . . to feel nothing at all.

He looked over his shoulder at the clearing behind him; it was coming along, but there was still so much more to do. The land had been purchased with help from his father after he had been hired to teach English at a small high school in Jaffrey. Asa loved the historic little town. Emerson, Thoreau, and Kipling had all spent time here, and Willa Cather had lived here when she wrote *My Antonia*—she was even buried in the local cemetery. Asa's parents had been thrilled with his new position and had driven up on several occasions to visit and see the parcel along the Contoocook River. The "Took," as locals called it, was one of the few rivers in New Hampshire that flowed north, escaping into the solace of the New England countryside, and Asa felt a kinship with its placid waters. He ran a calloused hand through his hair and rubbed his aching shoulders. Clearing brush was slow, tedious work, but he didn't mind. His brother had drawn up plans for a modest cabin with a center fieldstone chimney, and Asa looked forward to spending the New England winters next to its fireplace, but, for now, all he had was an Adirondack chair and a rustic fire pit. He had grown to love the mountains, and he no longer missed the ocean as much as he once had.

He had returned to Cape Cod only once after Noelle died. Isaac had asked him to be his best man at his wedding, and the small ceremony and reception had been held at the Chatham Bars. To everyone's surprise, Isaac had fallen head over heels in love with the redhead from college. After graduation, he had taken her out to the Cape, and as they walked along the moonlit beach, he had asked her to marry him.

The next day, Isaac had driven to New Hampshire. The two brothers had hiked Monadnock, and Asa had stood at the top quoting Emerson—" '*Monadnoc is a mountain strong . . . Tall and good my kind among; But well I know, no mountain can . . . Measure with a perfect man*' "—and Isaac had interrupted him to tell him the news. Asa had been speechless. He couldn't believe that his brother had finally settled down, but he had met Nina on several occasions, and he knew she would keep him in line. Asa had smiled broadly and continued: " '*Mute orator! Well skilled to plead . . . and send conviction without phrase . . . Thou dost supply the shortness of our days . . . And promise, on thy Founder's truth . . . long morrow to this mortal youth.*' " And then he had shook his brother's hand, clapped him on the back, and said he would be honored.

Asa set the book down on the arm of his chair and made a mental note to lend it to Isaac. Maybe he'd even buy him a copy for his birthday. He pulled himself from the chair, walked over to the river, reached into an icy pool, and fished out a bottle. He opened it, watched the sun slip behind the trees, and pictured Nauset Light—far away from where he stood. He knew, at that very moment, the faithful lighthouse was casting its light through the evening sky; he thought of his boyhood dream of being a lighthouse keeper and he smiled. Asa's thoughts were interrupted by a sound behind him. He turned in time to see his brother trying to sneak up on him. Realizing that he had been caught, Isaac burst into song. Asa grinned and Isaac nodded at the bottle. "Looks like I'm just in time."

Asa handed Isaac his untouched beer and reached into the river for another one. He opened it, tapped it against Isaac's, and took a sip. "So, how's fatherhood?"

Isaac sat in Asa's chair and smiled. "Great!"

He and Nina had wasted no time starting a family. He took out a picture of a rosy-cheeked cherub with strawberry-blond locks and showed it to his brother. "She's so good—never cries, smiles all the time, and loves to laugh. Thank goodness she doesn't take after her moody uncle."

Asa sat on a stump near the chair and looked at the picture. "Thank goodness she doesn't take after her funny-looking father."

Isaac glanced at the book on the arm of the chair. "Are you reading this?"

"Just finished—thought you might like to read it."

"Already have. The story of Howard Roark is on the unauthorized reading list for architecture students." He glanced around at the clearing. "It's looking good. When do you hope to break ground?"

"Two weeks, if all goes well." Asa paused. "What brings you up here anyway?"

"Dad sent me." Asa watched his brother look out at the river and waited for him to continue. "Asa, Uncle Nate had a heart attack."

Asa stared. "Is he okay?"

Isaac shook his head. "No, Asa . . ."

Asa looked at the last rays of sunlight filtering through the trees and absently wiped at the condensation on his bottle. He realized that the only other time he had seen Nate, after Noelle's funeral, was at Isaac's wedding. Isaac had pointed him out from across the room. His hair had turned snow white, and Asa had hardly recognized him. Nate had made his way over to greet them, and Asa had felt a wave of shame as he grasped Nate's firm, honest handshake. He had searched Nate's eyes—they still sparkled, but he knew they had seen more than their share of sorrow.

Over the years, Sarah had occasionally mentioned the little boy, Noah. She had reported that he was walking, then starting school, growing like a weed, and she had quietly told Asa that he should come home and see him. But Asa had stayed away— from the memory, from anything that reminded him of Noelle.

At the wedding, Asa had asked Nate about his son, and Nate had slipped a recent photo from his wallet. Asa had studied the picture and said, "He has Noelle's eyes." Nate had looked at Asa in an odd way. "Do you think so?"

Asa had nodded and, with tears in his eyes, started to excuse himself, but Nate had put his hand on his shoulder.

"Asa . . . ," he had said gently, "it's okay. . . ."

"Asa," Isaac interrupted his thoughts. "You need to come home."

## 102

Samuel stood at the railing in a pressed white oxford and black slacks. He looked out at the endless procession of whitecaps rushing toward the shore. Swirling his glass, he took a sip and whispered, "This one's for you, old pal." He looked around one last time at the vase of blue hydrangea blossoms on the linen tablecloth and mentally checked his list of preparations. He glanced from the old metal tub full of ice and bottles to the oak side table set with glasses and mixers.

Long ago, he and Nate had agreed that if anything ever happened, the one who was left behind would make sure that the other's life would be remembered—and celebrated—with a traditional gathering. Samuel could hear the sounds of Tommy Dorsey's band drifting out through the kitchen window and remembered that the chowder was still simmering on the stove. He had had a new helper with the clams this year, and his new helper had even known to rinse the clams. Samuel smiled as tears rolled down his cheeks. "You were a good dad," he whispered.

An hour later, Samuel looked around at the many friends

who had gathered to honor Nathaniel Shepherd. He looked at Sarah and the slight, blond-haired boy holding her hand. "Forgive me," he began, "if I don't get through this"—he ran his thumb under each eye—"without a few tears. I know Nate wanted it to be a celebration, but hopefully he will forgive me." He paused again, blinked, and bit his lip. "This gathering is not the same today without Nate, although I know he is with us in spirit. I always thought Nate and I would be sipping gin and tonics together in our rocking chairs." Those gathered chuckled warmly. "But I guess that is not to be . . ." Tears welled up in Samuel's eyes again, and he pressed his lips together in a half-smile, fighting them back. "Instead, the good Lord has seen fit to bring Nate home, and He couldn't have a finer servant. Nate was the best friend a man could ask for—kind and generous, loving and forgiving." Samuel looked around and saw Isaac standing by the door and then realized that Asa was standing beside him.

Tears spilled down Samuel's cheeks as he struggled to continue. "Nate weathered much sorrow, bittersweet sorrow, but . . . through it all, his faith was unwavering." He looked down and smiled, through his tears, at the small boy watching him. "But Nate knew joy too—immeasurable joy." Samuel wiped his eyes. "Okay, enough." He held up his glass, and everyone else did the same. "To our dear old friend . . . may God bless him . . ."

The voices joined together in the melancholy toast. . . .

"To Nate . . .
'Tis the chowdah that waarms a man's belly . . .
But aye, 'tis the gin that waarms his soul!"

# ∽ 103 ∾

Asa stood silently, watching the ebbing tide. He noticed a circular formation of old bricks being revealed by the tide. As he watched, the wet sand gently blanketed the edges of the worn edifice, and then the waves washed the sand away again. It had been years since Asa had walked along this beach, years since he had stood in this spot, but he was certain that the old foundation had not been visible when he was a boy.

"I thought I'd find you here," a quiet voice said.

Asa looked up and saw his father standing beside him.

Asa nodded. He motioned to the bricks. "Was that always there?"

"I suspect it's been there for a very long time," Samuel answered, "but time and erosion have now made it more visible."

"It looks like the foundation of a lighthouse."

Samuel nodded. "I'm sure it's from one of the Three Sisters."

They stood in silence for a while and watched as more of the foundation was exposed. Finally, Samuel said, "I have something for you." Asa looked up, and Samuel handed him a book. Asa took it and smoothed down a small tear in the cover.

"It was with Nate's papers," Samuel began, watching his son. "Asa, I knew Nate better than anyone, but it's impossible to know someone completely. Sometimes a person doesn't even know himself." He paused and looked back at the foundation. "But, Asa, God knows . . . He knows what we do before we do it. He knows what we say before we say it, and He forgives us—long before we are ready to forgive ourselves." Samuel paused again and looked at his son. "And then . . . Asa . . . God goes one step further and continues to bless us—no matter what we have done."

Samuel hesitated. "Asa, I don't know what happened all those years ago. I don't know what led Noelle and you into such a tragic situation. After all this time, though, you continue to stand there, angry at God for what you believe he has taken away, and, I think, angry at yourself for being a part of it. But, Asa, have you ever stopped being angry long enough to consider all that He has given you?"

Samuel turned to walk away, and Asa looked after him. "Dad . . ." Samuel turned back. "I'm sorry." Samuel smiled sadly and nodded.

Asa looked down again at the cover of the book. He remembered it well—the simple illustration of a tree on a brown background. He opened the cover and he saw his father's inscription:

> *For Asa,*
> *On the occasion of your*
> *Nineteenth Birthday!*
> *Enjoy!*
> *Much Love,*
> *Dad*

He turned the page, and an ivory-colored envelope fell out onto the sand. He picked it up and brushed it off. A sudden wind rushed down the beach and threatened to steal it from his hands, but he held it tightly and stared at the familiar elegant handwriting. His heart raced as he slipped out the thin paper. Tucked inside was a faded bus ticket dated June 21, 1961, and behind the ticket an old photograph. Asa stared in disbelief. *I wondered what had become of this.* Tears filled his eyes as remembered the night long ago. *She was so beautiful . . . and look at me—I was so young.*

He tucked the picture and the ticket back between the pages and carefully unfolded the delicate stationery. He glanced at the Howe Library letterhead in wonder and slowly read the words that had been so carefully chosen. . . .

> *My Dearest Asa,*
>
> *If you are reading this, then something has happened to me because it is with you that I long to be . . .*
>
> *Oh, Asa, if you only knew how much I miss you. You are in my heart every day, and I pray that you are managing. I will never forget the look in your eyes the last time I saw you. I am so very sorry that you found out that way. I hope that you can forgive me.*
>
> *As I write these words now, I am sitting in the Howe Library, praying that you will come through the door. I have wanted for so long to say these words to you and to see your face. I wonder if you will smile . . . Asa, I don't know what will become of us. I don't know all the answers, but I do know that the beloved child I carry is yours. I didn't know it at first—I wouldn't let myself believe it—but now, the scent of my body reminds me of you, and*

*somehow, deep in my heart, I realize I have always known.*

*I wish that I could stay until you do come through that door.*

*Asa, please forgive me and know that I will always love you.*

*Forever,*
*Noelle*

Asa stared at the words, trying to grasp the impact they would have on his life. With trembling hands, he read the letter again, savoring each word and allowing the bittersweet memory of the summer long ago to gently fill his mind. He looked at the signature—the promise to love forever—and realized that the passage of time had eased his sadness. As the sun set behind him, Asa looked back at the lighthouse set high on the rugged embankment. He watched its red and white light flash across the darkening sky, and he thought about the steady measurement of time. Every moment he had lived, every breath he had drawn, every night as he slept, the light had turned, without ceasing. . . .

# EPILOGUE

Asa turned and saw two figures making their way toward him. The taller of the two, he knew, was Maddie. He watched the smaller figure stoop to pick something up and run to the water to rinse it. Asa smiled, remembering the pockets full of smooth stones and sea glass he had collected as a boy. As they drew near, Asa knelt down and the boy ran toward him, clutching the treasure in his fist.

"Look at this stone," the boy exclaimed. "It's the shape of a heart."

"You're right," Asa said, holding it in his palm and watching the expression of delight on the boy's tan face. *He does look like his mother,* he thought.

The boy peered up at Asa with solemn eyes the color of the sweet summer sky and said, "You can have it."

Asa blinked back tears. "Thanks . . . I'll keep it for good luck." He paused. "I have something to show you too." Maddie stood by and watched them. "Do you see those old bricks?" Asa asked.

The boy nodded.

"That's the foundation of an old lighthouse."

The boy studied the worn circle and slipped his hand into Asa's, drawing him out for a closer look. As a wave rushed in, Asa felt the boy's small hand grip his more tightly. Asa looked back at Maddie and she smiled. He studied her hazel eyes and the sprinkle of freckles on the bridge of her nose, and he thought of the summer day, long ago, when she had stopped him in the rain and asked him if his name was Asa. Maddie had become his friend when he needed one most, and they had remained good friends throughout college. Asa smiled at her now and thought of the surprised look on her face when he had asked her to come to the Cape with him, realizing he had been just as surprised when she said yes.

Asa held out his free hand and Maddie took it. After a while, the threesome turned and walked slowly toward the wooden steps that climbed the sheer face of the fragile coastline. Out of habit, Asa silently counted the treads as he went up, but Noah, who was bounding ahead, counted out loud.

At the top, Asa looked up at the vastness of the night sky and spotted a familiar constellation.

"Noah, do you know what the Milky Way is?"

The boy nodded. "It's thousands of faint stars."

"That's right," Asa said, smiling. "Do you know which constellation is Cygnus, the Swan?"

Noah shook his head this time, and Asa pointed up at the stars.

"The best time to see it is right after your birthday. Do you see where the Milky Way begins to separate?" Noah nodded and Asa continued. "Just below and to the left is a large perfect cross with a bright star on the far side. That is Cygnus, the Swan, and the bright star is called Deneb, the Swan's tail." Asa looked over at Maddie and saw that she was studying the sky too. "There is a place inside the Swan—just to the left of the middle star where there are no faint stars—and that is called the

Coal Sack. Funny name, isn't it?" Noah nodded and slipped his hand into Asa's. Just as he did, a bright star shot out of the darkness and raced across the Milky Way.

"Look," Noah whispered, "a shooting star!"

Asa watched the star and then looked in wonder at the child by his side. "Pretty neat, Noah. I think God must have sent that for you."

Noah nodded solemnly and said, "For you too."

Asa smiled and gently squeezed his son's hand.

# Acknowledgments

Writing a novel takes a tremendous leap of faith—financially, temporally, and emotionally. Who knows what the outcome will be? When I'm writing, I often pray for guidance and I even ask God to send signs of reassurance.

One summer morning, after I'd just finished writing the passage in the book about the female cardinal, I was sitting on my front porch asking for assurance that all would be well. At the very moment of my prayer, a female cardinal flew by my head, through the open door into our mudroom, and fluttered around until she landed on the top frame of the bottom window in the bathroom. I followed her and without thinking unlatched the window, hoping she would fly out. But as soon as I did, I remembered that the spring in the window wasn't hooked properly. I watched in horror as the upper window slid down, taking the little cardinal with it! I stared in disbelief. *What had I done?* There she was trapped, upside down, between the two windows! Without thinking (again) about possible injury, I pushed the window up, and up she came with it! Shaken but seemingly unharmed, she found her way back outside. In astonishment and wonder, I sank into my chair. It was one sign of many that I will never forget.

I am thankful to my family and friends, who, through the years, have shaped my life and filled it to overflowing with rich memories. To Bruce, my husband and best friend, who has supported me every step of the way; and to our boys, Cole and Noah, who continually keep track of how many pages I've written and encourage me to do better. They are my inspiration! To my mom and dad, who never doubted for a second that I would publish a novel.

I'm forever indebted to my dad's neighbor, Mr. Jim Brownell, who put me in touch with my agent, Deirdre Mullane. I'm very thankful for Deirdre's help and guidance. Finally, I must thank Audrey LaFehr, my editor at Kensington Books, and everyone at Kensington who is working to make my dream come true.

The original Gin & Chowder Club still meets in the sleepy little town of Colebrook, Connecticut. I was just starting college when I first saw one of their fancy invitations, and although I never knew their purpose or pastime, I remember thinking that the name would be a wonderful title for a novel.

# THE GIN & CHOWDER CLUB

## Nan Rossiter

## ABOUT THIS GUIDE

The suggested questions that follow
are included to enhance your group's
reading of *The Gin & Chowder Club*.

# DISCUSSION QUESTIONS

1. From the very beginning the reader is aware that there is a strong physical attraction between Noelle and Asa. Are there any other (subconscious) factors that might have contributed to Noelle initiating an intimate relationship?

2. Asa has been raised to have a strong faith in God. He knows right from wrong and he struggles with the immorality of his desire for Noelle. Despite his faith and good conscience, he shamelessly betrays his father's best friend. How does this happen?

3. Noelle professes to love both Nate and Asa. Is it possible to truly love two people? Is it possible to be unfaithful to someone you truly love?

4. At what point do you think Nate suspects that the relationship between Noelle and Asa has become intimate? Do you think he is ever certain? Why doesn't he confront her?

5. Noelle struggles with overwhelming guilt and remorse. In her mind, how does she justify her actions?

6. What are some clues in the text that might lead the reader to surmise that Noah cannot be Nate's son?

7. After Noelle dies in childbirth, Asa turns his back on God. Is he angry with God or angry at himself? Is any-

one to blame for the tragedy? Does God punish sin, or does He bless us in spite of sin?

8. Nate loves Noah and raises him as his own. Why does he do this? What does it say about his character?

9. At what point do you think Samuel and Sarah suspect that Noah is Asa's son? Can you imagine their conversation?

10. Asa sees Nate for the last time at Isaac's wedding reception. After seeing a picture of Noah, Asa tearfully excuses himself, but Nate stops him and says, "It's okay." What does he mean when he says this?

11. After reading Noelle's letter, do you think she was planning to leave Nate? If so, why did she go back home?

12. In the end, Asa discovers that he is already forgiven— and blessed! Do you think he will be a good father?

13. Are the lives of Asa and Noah—and Maddie—potential book material???